T0160788

Angel Station

Jáchym Topol

ANGEL STATION

Translated from the Czech by Alex Zucker

DALKEY ARCHIVE PRESS

Originally published in Czech by Hynek as *Anděl* in 1995.

Copyright © 1995 by Jáchym Topol
Translation copyright © 2017 by Alex Zucker
First Dalkey Archive edition, 2017.

Library of Congress Cataloging-in-Publication Data
Names: Topol, Jáchym, 1962- author. | Zucker, Alex, translator.
Title: Angel station : a novel / by Jáchym Topol ; translated from the
Czech by Alex Zucker.
Other titles: Anděl. English
Description: First Dalkey Archive edition. | Victoria, TX : Dalkey
Archive Press, 2017.
Identifiers: LCCN 2016054004 | ISBN 9781943150120 (pbk. : alk.
paper)
Subjects: LCSH: Working class men--Czech Republic--Fiction.
Classification: LCC PG5039.3.O648 A8513 2017 | DDC
891.8/636--dc23
LC record available at https://lccn.loc.gov/2016054004

www.dalkeyarchive.com
Victoria, TX / McLean, IL / Dublin

MINISTRY OF CULTURE
CZECH REPUBLIC

This translation was subsidized by the Ministry of Culture of the Czech
Republic.

Dalkey Archive Press publications are, in part, made possible through
the support of the University of Houston-Victoria and its programs in
creative writing, publishing, and translation.

Printed on permanent/durable acid-free paper

Our soul is escaped as a bird
out of the snares of the fowlers:
the snare is broken,
and we are escaped.
Psalm 124:7

1. Baby Jesus Stolen

THERE WAS LIGHT above the buildings. High up in the faraway sky, falling in strips, then in a seamless layer, the solid white curtain slammed down into the city, swallowing it up, shrouding it from the universe, it fell suddenly, snapping down like a shop window blind.

Then the sky turned red and the light streamed down from the sun. It fell in between buildings, shining on buildings within buildings too, tumbling into cellars, blazing in courtyards, thrusting down light wells, it was everywhere.

It was cold, it was winter, and they were all living in it, the real ones as well as the ones only now hatching in the diseased imagination of the stammering storyteller as he mixed up the plot, the people and years, sitting over a drink in the Nonstop.

It was cold, Christmas was drawing near, and on Holy Night it happened, Christmas Eve, that Blessed Day . . . the melee at St. Bruno's Church. It was only afterward that Elephanta cursed the foreign clan and Laci got his new name.

It was Holy Mass and the Gypsy women from Romania stood at the head of the throng. Illuminated by the candles, the coins sewn to their coats and blouses, the long black hair beneath their bandanas, gleamed in the furtive light as they looked on in rapture . . . all of them, drawn to the church by the power of the Black Dahlia, stood there along with the other residents of the neighborhood, the longtime inhabitants who went to church regularly, watching, some no doubt with a dash of contempt, as the former chief of militia fervently crossed himself, all the local party bosses had turned out for the big night, prominent businessmen, wheeler-dealers of every stripe, the cream of Smíchov, people who'd moved to the area only recently and people whose grandparents had known Klestka the smuggler and called him by name . . . and a man named Li stood off in the corner, because there had been a change in his life.

Whenever Li searched within himself, he was sure he'd become a monster. But suddenly pain had entered his life and turned it upside down. So badly he didn't know what to do with himself . . . and now here he was, squeezed in with the others.

Lyuba was there too, with great hope inside her, leaning against the church wall, lightly, just her elbow, she was there with the rest of them, the snowy dampness steaming off of all the coats and dresses, and Guinea Pig was also there . . . standing next to Lyuba, but they were oblivious to each other . . . Guinea Pig's granny had promised him, for the holidays, okay . . . but then it's back to the Home, and no ifs, ands, or buts, so he'd given her the nod . . . he had his eye on the Nativity scene, wondering if that stuff sparkling on the saints' hats was really gold, he'd talked it over awhile in front of the church with Laci, his running buddy from the video arcades, but that was before they'd known that tonight the little shooter would get a new name.

Standing there with the rest of them too was a man who for a long time had been nothing but a number; then he'd gotten a name and an assignment. He wasn't there of his own free will; he'd been sent. Now he stood there among the believers, feeling the touch of many bodies against his shoulders and back for the first time in a long while.

Little old ladies sat in the pews, little old ladies and little old men, trundled in on a special bus from the retirement home, some rich foundation had sprung for the trip, so now they sang its praises . . . and crammed in there along with them were dolled-up hookers from Sexyland Dinah and their gold chain–draped beaus, passing bottles around, but on the sly, they kept their mouths shut . . . they'd come because it was the proper

thing to do nowadays, in the new times . . . in Smíchov. Dead
Monkey was there too, with his lover, Ládínek, the one who'd
set a whore on fire, that time . . . no one had pinned it on him,
so it was safe for him to be there, Monkey had thrown him for
a roll in the snow outside and now Ládínek stood steaming
white, the moisture rising off him in wisps . . . a sizable number
of people were there, it was a diverse crowd . . . Elephanta was
a bit jealous of her Romanian relatives, the women, in their
bright-colored blouses, attracted a lot of attention . . . but she
was sure of her power, only she had spoken directly to the Black
Dahlia, who had told them all . . . to come, and here they were.
Elephanta kept quiet for now, her giant infected foot sandwiched
in between the pews . . . tomorrow she would be back, lording
it over the intersection by Angel Station, standing and ambling
around, wielding the invisible reins of power, settling feuds and
straightening out crooked fortunes. For instance with some acid
in an evil eye.

A reporter, waiting there because he'd paid a tidy sum for a
confidential tip that the President himself might turn up, briefly
and unannounced . . . only the source who'd tipped him off was
all dried up and he didn't know it . . . stepped aside. Elephanta
frightened him. But her performance was yet to come. He didn't
know he would end up writing his article about her.

The priest appeared. No one, not even he himself, suspected
he was a descendant of the learned and wise man whose vision
had given a name to the nearby intersection on whose corners
and around whose trapdoors the neighborhood's life played
out. But just then Laci disturbed the peace, as he had been
trained to whenever he spotted anything that wasn't nailed
down . . . he snatched up the vessel of holy water believers were
dipping their fingers into and bolted, stupid Mass, what did he
care. A commotion broke out by the entrance. Laci's mother,
one of the Romanian Gypsies, elbowed her way through the
crowd, sending a stir through the rows, the older congregation
members, weak in the knees, toppling to every side. Laci

ducked and dodged, but the sexton grabbed hold of him, Laci's
momma caught him as he raced to her with the booty . . . to
hide beneath her skirts . . . and pasted a couple of slaps across
his startled face. He was stunned, nobody'd ever said, not in
church, it's not allowed . . . from then on, though, he knew . . .
he burst out sobbing. The area in front of St. Bruno, across the
street from the Savings Bank, filled up with a throng of angry
men, the locals, incensed at the blatant offense, were one step
away from attacking their relatives, who had come from the
mountains to the city, how could they be refused, after all . . .
and were now living ten and fifteen at a time with the established
residents, at one fell swoop the sacrilege threatened to unleash
the old feuds . . . Elephanta, with her gigantic swollen foot,
shoved her way outside . . . screaming curses at the Romanians
and to go the hell back where they came from . . . pulled up as
the scribbler caught her in his flash, made a lunge for him . . .
he slipped, cracked his head on the step in front of the church,
the one where foundlings had once been laid, he was bleeding,
it had to be dealt with . . . just then, one of Laci's older sisters in
front of the altar, either gone amok or enlightened by the Spirit,
started writhing and screaming at the foot of the flower-strewn
statue of Mary, and the rest of her relatives wasted no time
in joining in . . . screaming because they knew what awaited
them back in the mountains, with no money, no passports,
tore off their hoods and bandanas, let down their hair, spinning
in place, rolling their heads, stomping their feet, black locks
whirling as they danced, skidding over the candle flames, and
the church's fragrance of holy wood and incense gave way to the
distinctive smell of singed hair, shrieking . . . later they would
claim that the Virgin Mary had spoken to them and that her
speech had been exceedingly sweet . . . and encouraging . . .
pouring out a barrage of screams, some of the Gypsy women
pounded their heads against the cold stone of the church floor,
their pleas to Mary blending with the oldest of invocations, the
other Christians backing away, jostling one another . . . the

people in the front rows squeezed toward the exit, but the ones by the door didn't want to miss out on the fun, the Romanian women who weren't by the altar joined in at least with applause, the local politicians and other dignitaries were getting nervous, and a few people stood up from the pews and comically craned their heads as though looking for an usher, they couldn't get out now with the crowd shoving past the pews, this way and back again, they couldn't get away . . . suddenly the priest raised his hands . . . and the Gypsy women quieted down, trading furtive winks perhaps, bowing their heads and gazing up through the candles at Mary, who had come to their aid, after all she was one of theirs . . . in the soft haze of the smoking flames she looked black, just like them . . .

Laci returned the sacred vessel to the sexton, who began scolding him but then fell silent, noticing it was full of bills, and the dark, silent men stuffed his pockets with them too, the men in mustaches slapping him on the back, continuing to feed him cash until he stopped his fuming . . . but then, when Mass was over, when the whole thing was done and the people had gone their way, he discovered someone had stolen the Baby Jesus, the neighborhood's wooden Christ Child, out of the crèche.

Or at least that was how the night's scandal sounded later on . . . from the mouth of the mixed-up storyteller, the pathological liar sitting there in the Nonstop, and he also told about Hooks, who walked around the neighborhood, walking and watching . . . looking to see . . . some people, y'know, they got friends they can call anytime, night or day, said the storyteller, and he blinked . . . some people got prayers an some people, shit, they got nothin . . . and he told about the air shafts too, the air shafts in every building around, where you hear so much you're better off listening to the radio, he said . . . before coming to the end of his spurious tale of Hooks, who knew that whoever takes a drug, becomes the drug . . . and then they're dead . . . a twisted tale from the chronicles of Prague's fifth district, a cock-and-bull story, pure phantasmagoria, a tale of eye disease

in a state of advanced psychopathy and of the desire to find bliss
in the here and now . . . a kind of morality play with ghosts,
a bedtime story to tell the scamps . . . he also told about the
pit that swallows people up, jabbing a dirty finger toward the
window at his back . . . an what with all that an everything else
what do you do . . . he said beneath the fluorescent lamps with a
chemical sky writhing up above . . . and he spoke to me of pain,
and the beastly pain that cuts you down in the blink of an eye,
like a sudden gust of wind, we looked out the glass wall of the
Nonstop at Angel Station . . . and then it was light again, red
skies . . . a new day.

2. The Windows

Hooks blinked. But it didn't go away. He could see it, the blood, like a red honeycomb, like a membrane, in his left eye. Then in his right. The blood poured from the sky, falling into his eyes. He had an instinct to duck out of the way, huddle his body around the red spot spreading across his retina, wrap his muscles, tendons, bones, hair around it somehow, everything that he knew beyond a doubt belonged to him, and dissolve the vision inside him.

He soon realized it was best to avoid the window, all windows. As long as he kept his gaze turned in toward the room, the crimson didn't flare up, he saw people, men, their shadows. And didn't look out the windows.

He remembered quite clearly the first time the vision had come.

He'd been standing at the intersection waiting for a tram when the sky coagulated. He sidestepped the people crowding onto the tram and looked. Watched the low cumuli in the slow-moving sky above Angel Station, saw them run through with a crimson vein, outlined in silver. Then the fleecy clouds let loose the red, caught him in the eyes, he'd had to lean against a lamppost.

The sky was red. It was dazzling. He tried to move, felt a drip, drop, drip on his shoulders, neck, scalp, knew it was blood.

Then he went on the lam. Took off. Away from his turf. But the red flashes had found him.

Here he'd made a habit of staying away from the barred windows, even when the frost coated them in Arctic maps, covering up the sky, the vision was inside him still and the jagged frost might have conjured up the image of a polar bear bleeding on fresh-fallen snow. Or something. Those kinds of fantasies he was happy to give up.

He wandered the corridors. Shuffled his feet. Got used to it. His first time here he'd been ceaseless, sleepless even after the nth Rohypnol. They gave him some other chemical. He woke up screaming, woke the others, caused a disturbance. Then the shots hit the spot. And at last he sank into dreams. Awful ones. Colors and monsters tumbling over one another, and crimson always came out on top. The unmistakable crimson of blood-soaked clouds from the planet Chaos.

And the faces. It wasn't until later that he figured out what the red was. Where the overeager parts of his brain got it from and what released it into his scleral cells.

Now he fell asleep, sinking into himself and seeing the faces. Mostly the kind he could just as soon do without meeting.

They were the sort of faces every tram is full of, every reading room, laundromat, any snack bar or swimming pool, as if his brain were replaying every encounter he'd ever had, especially the fleeting ones from the streets, the subway. Faces.

The tour would begin with faces from the neighborhood, first to float in usually was the shopkeeper's ugly mug, then women, more women, assorted moms, eventually it dawned on him which cash registers, corner stores, tram stops he'd seen them at, moms with shopping bags, with kids, then he glided past the faces of his buddies, some he only knew from the waist up anyway, hunkered down in the pub in his dream, tipping back pints, he saw the quick-witted Not Much and the dazzling Madla from SuperDrug, there was Steffi the scrawny waitress, leaning out the window, and her little sister, Dora the bitch, the famous Telebingo winner, he spotted faces he recognized or semi-recognized from the street, fellow bus riders, the familiar strangers from the daily commute, a woman beautiful as a battleship, who he'd met five years ago in the fall, the faces in his drowsy brain changing one into the next, like a rotating picture flashing across endless walls of crystal, then suddenly one of the eyes in the dream would come to a stop right in front of his eye, flicker, and the vein of red running through the white would burst, oozing blood. And the blood slowly engulfed the picture. Flowing from the clouds and flowing from the faces, flowing toward him, he was sure.

In the daytime he was scared to blink his left eye, that was where the vision usually began. Apart from that, he kept his cool, didn't talk to anyone. But he'd spoken to start out with, just a word or two here and there, to keep up appearances.

He paced the corridors designated for it. Ate off a plate whenever the staff slid one in front of him. Washed the floor when he got a rag. Gave coherent answers during doctors' rounds. Unquestioned, he said nothing.

To the glad-handers and other meddlesome types he made it plain he was not to be disturbed. They thought he was crazy. He sat, stared, lay, stood, ate, now even slept too. At first he suffered pangs of guilt over Lyuba, but his proud resolution, which, though he didn't realize it, he shared with approximately 70 percent of the wack jobs, fruitcakes, basket cases, and other patients—namely, that he'd just get his act together and head back out into the streets, into the world, and especially back to her, Lyuba, to make amends for his obvious faults and indiscretions—that resolution kept him on his feet.

He made up his mind not to sink any lower, and did his best to steer clear of the people in whom he could sense the gaping abyss, of course in such a way so as to avoid the windows if possible. The ones who reeked of the abyss had no resolutions left, either that or they kept them hidden deep inside themselves, in a pit of pain, in a salty ocean of tears occasionally rippled by waves or whipped by hurricanes of hysteria. They lived a life of medication-dulled desperation. He could sense it. Passing them by in his tracks across the trampled linoleum, circling, always circling, in his hospital-issue slippers that went flip, flop, flip.

Maybe I oughta go see the eye guy, said Hooks, blinking

into the darkness in the corner, nah, screw it, my problems're of a mental nature, he diagnosticated. It didn't occur to him until later that what he saw was really there and that only he could see it.

This wasn't his first stay on the ward. But it was the first time he'd driven up to the hospital gates of his own free will, and in a cab no less.

He kept only what was essential for his hygienic needs, or at least what he considered essential, in a bag labeled Air France. The rest of his stuff he'd dumped in a trash can at the intersection. Wouldn't grow mold in there, that's for sure. He gave no thought to his unwitting good deed.

The first bum to grab one of his French souvenirs and pull it out into the light rewarded Hooks from a distance with a crazy, incredulous smile. He didn't give a damn. He had already hit bottom.

Even when Hooks had tried to run, the vision had caught up with him. It was waiting here too. And the view of the sky here was particularly grim. The vision had come again, mercilessly. Just as he was on his way to see her, Lyuba, firmly resolved this time to become a happy man.

The vision of blood had come and cut him down. By the trams again, at the noisy, dirty intersection. Angel Station. The pit. Just like before. It had been all he could do just to make the trip here, to the ward.

They'd taken him in, why not. Not exactly with open arms, but he looked needy enough. He looked awful. They wanted to know what sort of troubles he was having. Some he said, some he didn't. They asked his address: he gave Lyuba's. Explained the marks on his arms. They smiled. He squinted through the whole interview, but not a peep about the red, about the blood from the clouds. The only person he called, eventually, was his old friend Brownie. His buddy, he hoped.

After the evening feed, Hooks would sit by the bathrooms

in the room reserved for nicotine and the blabbermouths whom even the nightly dose of meds couldn't put to sleep.

This was where the inventive types congregated, the resourceful under-the-tonguers who pretended to swallow their pills but instead saved them up and sold them to the others, priced by size and color, the liars and the fibbers who needed to confess, even if only to the walls, and the more carvings and scrawls that appeared on those walls, spattered brown with the clotted blood of somebody's farewell party, the more urgent the pleas of the endlessly tormented and the con men's crazy sermons, weaving together or wailing solo . . . this was the place where the horny homos flocked, the greenhorns and the sissies too scared to sleep in the dormitory.

Dormitory, it was a warehouse . . . a white room kept locked tight during the day, clean as a scalpel and reeking of disinfectant, at nighttime it erupted with the darkest of predatory odors, the clammy smell of fear and the stench of decay . . . that was the old men who'd spent every night in there for decades, and sometimes there was an almost imperceptible acrid smell, narrow and thin, and that was insanity, weaving through the other smells like a black thread through the maze of embroidery on a kitschy tablecloth, confusing them, turning them inside out, twisting and turning through the other smells, swerving, dodging, it was almost as if it were feeding on them. The dormitory, a warehouse of up to sixty male bodies, most either restlessly tossing and turning, or lying in the most impossible positions, heads wracked with medication, bodies convulsed in a permanent cramp, like some scene from after a massacre.

Occasionally a nurse would come and break up the bunch by the bathroom, but most of the ones who gathered there were nuthouse vets, and the usual punishments, from revoking outdoor privileges to disciplinary speeches laced with the smell of burnt electrodes as the head doctor himself screws you with the juice, so keep that rubber in your teeth, now hold it in there, son, wouldn't want to lose that tongue . . . didn't upset any of them, except maybe the masochists, who would just as soon have told the nurse: I'm sorry, mommy! and handed over the scourge themselves.

The insomniacs were feasting on pills, one, right in front of Hooks, flirtatiously gummed a sneaker, trying to get his attention, while an ancient white-haired schizoid was swigging down the bug juice and in between scalding gulps shouting: Mine! and Mine! One greenhorn gestured to another like a high priest, speaking knowingly of life after death and how he had been there, a guy who'd fucked a goat paced from corner to corner, somebody was hiccuping, somebody was taking a shit, and somebody else was sobbing. Hooks left them all alone. In accordance with the law of the jungle, he took someone else's spot on the bench, as far from the window as possible, and kept his trap shut. Played with the threads prolapsing from the hem of his hospital gown like the slender intestines of some giant fairy-tale grasshopper (that was what he thought, but just to be safe he kept his metaphor to himself), and tried not to absorb the endless conversations and monologues of his fellow patients.

Right from the start he'd sworn to himself that not only would he not listen to them, but he didn't want to remember them. Not a word. Not a face. He tried to travel inside himself, grab hold of that first red thread somehow and pull himself into the red sediment that engulfed his brain, he wanted to trace his vision back to its origin and spook it, drive it out into the open, he wanted to know what it was, he wanted to know why, he longed not to go insane.

3. The Building

HOOKS HAD GROWN up in a library. Quite possibly that was why real life later seemed so difficult.

He longed for independence, and it might even be said: like hawks soaring through the autumn sky thirst for the unknown. Hawks of course, besides the cloudy membrane that so mysteriously veils their bleary eyes, also have wings and flight paths built into their genes; Hooks stood there, at a loss, with a creepy grin and two left hands.

He'd forgotten his childhood, slacked his way through his youth running from cops on instinct, somehow he'd survived his youth and traded it in for what he was now. The odd jobs he had all merged into one big blurry smudge of boredom, drudgery, and forced contact with people who either didn't interest him or, worse, were a pain in the ass. As much as possible he'd avoided work, tracking down life, peering around corners.

As for the parents he had once so eagerly watched from his crib—in a family of the type: father, mother, child (him)—he washed his hands of them before you could say "toy boat" three times fast.

They talked on the phone occasionally. Hooks would call from a booth. Usually when he needed something. Usually money. But he'd overdone it, and his parental support had been cut off as abruptly and inexorably as the family's ancient grandfather clock, which in Hooks's mind signified eternity, had one day ground to a halt. He knew that by taking an allowance, however negligible, at least he provided his parents with proof that he was alive. The moment the cash flow stopped, he logically concluded that the two of them didn't care whether he lived or died.

It happened one fall morning. A timid shadow detached itself from the furiously arguing figure in the phone booth. Hooks swore down the line as his girlfriend walked away. That had been the last one. A few months later, he couldn't even remember her name.

He stood in the phone booth alone. Alright then, he'd said to himself. Leaned against the glass, took a deep breath. He was yet to encounter loneliness, spiritual confusion, true cruelty, he was to get a whiff of death. A struggle with faith awaited him, he was to discover hope. All this awaited him, he didn't know it. But he had a hunch. It was in the air.

His new job had seemed pretty fun at first. He'd never come across anything like it in his reading. But he soon realized it was wretched work, worse than all the rest, the kind of work that takes only the most severe extremes from the pristine flames and squalid filth that go into it, and first scars, then destroys whoever stumbles into the furnaces' path. The guys who worked down in the factory basement were true lowlifes. At first he'd felt like a spy in enemy territory. Till it all ran together for him.

The first day, in his honor they said, they tossed a cat in the furnace. It didn't even yowl as the flames roared to life, consuming its scrawny body with a barely audible hiss. Hooks walked out. Considered leaving. Went back in. They made fun of him. There was no way to ignore them, so he made some comment back . . . they swept up the coal with rakes, a broom would've ignited at the first lump of glowing coal, bursting into flames like a torch. They'd explained that to him.

But he liked staring into the flames. The furnaces looked like ovens, built of fire-resistant brick and iron-plated. He liked watching the flames, liked jumping back from the blaze, the fiery tongue that came hissing out whenever he opened the hatch to feed the searing heat.

The books had stood on shelves around the walls of his

bedroom, level with the room's only window. It had always been dark in there, probably that was why mornings when he got up at four to go to work it reminded him of his childhood. He still remembered the dark.

It was grueling work, his hands were soon covered with calluses and blisters. Sometimes he would climb up on the platform over the furnaces with a book, but he couldn't concentrate. The other workers teased him for reading. One said only queers read books. They threw chunks of coke at him. Sometimes when he was up there he could see the white foam between the iron plates. Deposits from the toxic fumes. If he stayed up there too long, he could pass out.

The heat up top was suffocating, down below a cool breeze blew from the giant fans. If he hunched down right in the middle of the furnace, where the lightbulb hung on a wire from the ceiling, he felt stifling hot from his eyes up and his chin and cheeks were cold.

He walked out back, through the tunnel, to fetch the coal, clanging his shovel against the walls to scare away the rats. He quickly came to dislike the other workers even more than those ravenous beasts. They called him Screw-up, because he kept hurting himself. He didn't find it amusing, but he wasn't surprised.

Twenty wheelbarrows here, smoke, twenty wheelbarrows there, smoke, fifteen wheelbarrows there, and hold on, it's burning, stupid. Switch on the safety, not working . . . wait a sec, okay. Now take a breather. Lie down on some rags, stick a brick resourcefully wrapped in newspaper under your toxin-addled head. Just then, the pile of coke collapses on you.

The other workers switched his shifts, gave him low-grade coal, and one time they stole some money out of his coat pocket. They grinned as he gaped at the shrunken sum. The mythical heroes Hooks had once read about with such pleasure would have slain them on the spot.

He got himself a small room in a divided flat on Plzeňská

Street, a long thoroughfare lined with run-down, beat-up buildings. He gathered up his paltry belongings from the flats where he'd been sleeping, a couple friends', around, and hauled them into his new home.

The dirty, noisy street led to a feeder road that each day bore thousands of cars rumbling out of Prague.

He was up on the second floor, with a window onto the balcony that ran around the courtyard. He would've put bars on it if it had been up to him.

Inside the building it was permanently dark, the tenants stole the lightbulbs. One night as he groped his way up the creaky stairs, a shadowy figure darted out of the corner at him, seized him by the neck with powerful hands, and flung him to the ground. It was Machata, his neighbor who ran the shop downstairs. He stammered out an apology, more like a growl, stepped over Hooks, and slammed the door to his flat behind him.

On Saturday nights the street came to life, crews of Gypsies promenading, crowding into taprooms, weaving in and out of traffic, the women pushing baby carriages, shouting out to one another, passing bottles back and forth.

They're goin out to the movies, his neighbor said. Whatever village they dug em up in had a theater showed movies once a week, so it's like a habit of theirs, Machata the shopkeeper enlightened him.

Late mornings, when Hooks was still trying to sleep, the women out on the balcony ringing the courtyard would scream insults and obscenities at each other. Smash dishes. Argue over attic space, whose turn it was in the laundry room, whatever. Never again did Hooks hear the words cunt, whore, bitch, and dylina, delivered in a machine-gun staccato or a powerful, semi-sloshed bass, used with such frequency.

Red flags and banners hung here and there along their street, as they did on every other. lenin lives, now more than ever, and he will live on, as our conscience, our strength, and our weapon! declared a poster next to the building's front door. About a week after Hooks moved in, someone drew swastikas in Lenin's eyes and horns on top of his head. The first time he saw the devilized portrait, Hooks got worried. It might be for him. Since he'd just moved in. But the very next day someone tore it down. Leaving only the rusty thumbtacks. Before long, they were pinning something else in place. Whatever it was, he barely noticed. Nowhere else had he felt so immune to that tired propaganda. And nowhere else had he ever seen children battered so viciously. The neighbors' little girl got a beating almost like clockwork. Sometimes at night he could hear her cries.

What'm I sposta do? he thought, tossing in bed. I gotta get up at four a.m. I oughta say somethin to Machata . . . it's not like I can go to the authorities . . . if I turn em in, what'll they say, I'll lose the flat . . . they'll say I'm a pervert, they'll say . . . Hooks's teeth chattered. In the dark. The girl stopped screaming. He fell asleep.

Business was brisk, both in and around the building. Some days the courtyard would be stacked with crates, five or six burly guys lounging around on top of them. Their flashy, pseudo-suave clothing made them stand out in this neighborhood. But their drink-worn faces, muscular arms, and paunches bulging out of their white polyester shirts attested to their membership in the local underworld. They addressed the cops on the street by name. The women on the balcony, spent, shapeless old crones who spent their lives in factories and lines, merrily hollered down at them, inviting them up for beer.

I'm surrounded, Hooks thought. What do those old bags want with them . . . oh, those're their moms, take it easy, he said to himself.

In the hallway he tried to be polite, and always said hello first. His neighbors would look back at him, surprised and suspicious.

Any one of these characters could kick down my door an

stomp my face in, just for laughs. Maybe they think I'm an agent, or a spy from the competition, or maybe just off my rocker . . .

One day he noticed spatters of blood on the staircase. He walked around them but rubbed against the wall. The blood was there too. One day he opened the front door, guy came running out with a knife in his hand. Slammed into Hooks, knocked the paper bag out of his hand, it smashed on the steps, the bottles broke. Sometimes screams woke him at night, the neighbors, fighting or partying or both. He didn't get much sleep. Pills scared him, but he soon found he could get to sleep after a couple beers. In the time until he nodded off, the alcohol altered his senses, the noise from the courtyard, the slamming doors and curses, sounded like they came from another world, a world away.

For food he had a supply of cheap army rations. Purchased downstairs, of course. Sometimes he felt sick to his stomach. His job at the furnace drained him. One day a rat in the cellar bit him on the boot, he busted its spine with a shovel and smashed in its head. The next day the carcass was gone. Had the other guys cleaned it up, or was it just a hallucination? Maybe it was time to get back to the books. Is this a trap? Maybe I oughta find myself some other job, a new place to live. But how? Where?

Whenever Hooks ran into someone he knew, they ended up over beer. Where you been holed up? his buddies would ask. Where you at? Cops hasslin you?

A lot of people got locked up in those days. Including some he knew. Usually they didn't keep them for long. The powers-that-be were losing confidence; brutality was on the rise. At the factory they said one of the managers got caught at a demonstration, they drove him to the woods outside of Prague and beat his ass. Hooks could believe it. Čáp, a guy he'd met at the pub, got kicked in the head by the cops. They'd killed Mitlin's cousin. Soldiers shot him at the border, dragged him out of no-man's-land and left him to bleed to death in the middle of the Czech forest. There were whispers that the trials were starting up again.

The guys working the furnaces thought it was hilarious. They kept two cats down in the cellar, Liza and Mao they called them. Huge cats, rat killers, supposedly it was hormone shots that had made them so big. They were mutants. Mao had only one eye, with a deep scar where the other one should have been, the bald patch from the wound ran all the way up his forehead. Hooks knew by then what the men did with the kittens.

Sometimes at night, when he had a solo shift, he would climb up on the platform and toss chunks of salami down into the tunnel, the rats would start to swarm. He knew how it went from there: first Mao pounced, then Liza, then the killing began. The rats fell for it every time. Maybe they don't care, he thought. Maybe they realize someone's always got to pay the price. But meanwhile the rest get their fill. He walked out of the darkness and stifling heat and stood in the factory yard among the heaps of coal and iron, among the scrap. He would wait till the cats were gone to go back. He raised his head, the moon up above glowed dully in the silence.

One day at the intersection, he ran into Not Much, she was pushing a baby carriage. Underneath the kid she had a stack of flyers, gave him a few. He mischievously stuffed them into the mailboxes in his building. He'd seen the protests on TV at the pub where he sometimes went, the pub on the hill. Karla leaned across the table to him and whispered: Shorty went illegal! He's hidin out in Poland! But don't tell anyone, it's a secret . . . all sorts of rumors were going around . . . Just as soon as I settle in, get my act together, I'll lend a hand, Hooks told his pals . . . he was standing on Coal Market Square one day, underneath the scaffolding, when someone somewhere up above . . . shouted something, sheets of paper, flyers, came floating down onto the vendors' stalls like giant snowflakes . . . the street was suddenly full of cops, somebody somewhere ran for it, elbowing through the crowd, there was one tweet, then another, all the whistles blended together, Hooks sidestepped a guy reaching out to grab him, ducked down a passageway . . . Just as soon as I settle in, I'll come round the usual spots, Hooks assured his buddies at the pub . . . but today I gotta get goin, I got a job! You, a job? Yeah right.

But one day he stopped going to work. He had enough money to last awhile. His papers were in order for the time being, too. One morning he just didn't get out of bed. Flung the alarm clock against the wall, still half asleep, and woke up two days later.

Winter was coming. He needed to lay up coal in the cellar, but one of the other tenants had tossed his stuff out, into the water on the cellar floor, and padlocked the door. Hooks took an ax for chopping wood. Kept it under his bed. Walking downstairs, the handle solid in his hand, at the other end the metal blade, cold and naked, he didn't feel bad at all. He knocked off the lock, left it lying on the dirty floor, and put on his own. He started back up the stairs, but then turned around and went back. Kicked the lock, then hammered it with the dull end of the ax till it was nothing but a shapeless hunk of metal. He left it there on the floor for everyone to see.

On the balcony stood a young woman. Never seen her before. It was Lyuba.

Lookin for me? he asked.

I'm your neighbor, she said.

You takin the Machatas' place? he said, brightening up.

No, she smiled. Your neighbor from the other side.

C'mon in. If you want, said Hooks.

Hm, she said. She peered down from the balcony, the courtyard was empty. His grubby quilted jacket, even the ax, didn't rate a glance. She lit up a smoke, took a drag. She wore bright red lipstick. Her long black hair was tied in a bun held in place by a massive black barrette. She had rings on every finger. One of the silver bands was shaped like a spider, with eyes. The rings and the barrette, the heavy barbaric adornments, she wore them, it seemed to him, lightly. Her hair looked thick and rough. He had an urge to touch it.

Hooks found out from her that the old lady next door had died recently. He'd heard her cough sometimes. All these one-room dumps had been made by splitting flats in two. The Red Guards had evicted the bourgeoisie and divvied up their spacious flats with partitions. Just walled up the doors and moved in the poor folk. Once upon a time. Back in the day.

I had no idea, he said, setting up the hot plate. That she was dead. Would you like some tea?

Have you got anything to drink?

Beer.

Wait, I'll go grab some brandy.

Hooks wrestled with the hot plate, where had she come from? What did she want here? Her pale face . . . people around here didn't expect anything good from strangers, in fact they were mostly just plain scared of them. He tried to tidy up a bit, but it was pointless. Tossed his clothes under the bed, books on top of the wardrobe. He still had a few.

Housecleaning? She walked back in holding two glasses.

He found out her family used to own the buildings on this street. This divided flat was all the Communists had let them keep.

This was where the plant from the District Committee always lived, she stamped her heel on the floor. How'd you get in here?

Woke up one day and had nowhere to live. They gave it to me. Thanks to the psychiatrists.

Troubles?

Not really.

She'd left her husband, she said, but now that the flat had opened up, she was planning to move in. Had the papers for it and everything.

When did that lady die? Hooks asked.

She was lying in there a couple days. They just took her out today.

What? She didn't even smell. Or maybe I've got a cold, said Hooks.

She was my mother. But we didn't talk.

Sincere condolences, he said.

Seriously, she laid a hand on her heart, we hadn't seen each other in years. Her death means nothing to me. Maybe later I'll feel it.

If she did, she never said so. He noticed she had the flat repainted. He could smell the whitewashed plaster from his place.

Sometimes at night he would stand in front of the walled-up door, he couldn't believe a young woman was sleeping in there. A young woman like her. They would run into each other in the hallway. She often wore her hair in a bun.

Sometimes they'd stop and visit.

One night a fight broke out on the stairwell. Then the quarreling voices were drowned out by a woman's shrieks. Hooks, half asleep, heard a rap on the walled-up door. Lyuba was signaling him with her knuckles. It sounded more amused than alarmed. Can you say that about a knock? He rapped back. Then heard her voice.

You asleep? she said.

No.

You don't have to talk so loud. Come over here, it sounded as if her lips were right in his ear.

Things had been going downhill for Hooks. With no papers to prove he had steady employment, he was terrified of the police. With the law the way it was, they could easily lock him up. He usually put on workman's coveralls when he went out. It was the best disguise, and not only in his opinion. He avoided his friends, stayed away from the protests. He barely escaped a raid at the pub on the hill one day, and didn't dare go back. His new neighbor, Lyuba, intrigued him, the last thing he wanted now was to end up in jail for parasitism.

That night with Lyuba, and what came after it, was like manna from heaven.

When he walked through the halls of the building now, he tried to make like a shadow. From the shopkeeper's comments he gathered the neighbors knew he wasn't working. He was paranoid that they took him for an informer. At the same time he was afraid of being denounced and scared stiff of the secret police. He hardly ever went out. The saleslady in the shop down the street asked where he lived. Started making advances, slipping the expensive cheeses she kept under the counter into the paper sacks with his rolls. He had no choice but to pay for them. Machata slammed his cigarettes down on the counter without giving back his change. Hooks didn't have the nerve to ask for it. The old bags in the building didn't return his greetings and looked at him askance.

He would try to read, curled up in his lair. But the letters waged war on each other. The book's plot would get tangled up with the stories and characters in his head. And none of it made sense.

Is insanity making a play for me? he wondered sometimes, late at night. He tried to calm down by taking deep breaths . . . and then again sometimes he would exercise so frantically that he dropped to the floor in exhaustion.

He had opened the door to her flat that night and seen her lying in bed. The noise from out in the hallway grew more and more distant, until it ceased altogether.

Maybe his mania and her loneliness (no one ever visited her) merged into a single body. He assumed she understood what he said, she gave almost no reply. But they didn't do much talking. Toward morning, they made a bed on the floor to give themselves more room.

You might not believe me, she said. But when you came in I was still asleep. I dreamed you were walking into my dream, and then suddenly there you were.

But we knocked on the wall to each other. Thanks for that.

What?

Yeah, I guess you got scared by the fight, that racket outside.

What fight? What're you talking about?

Okay. Maybe I was the one that was dreaming. Anyway, doesn't matter.

Nope, not now, she said.

Lyuba, he said her name to himself over and over that night. Lyuba, Lyuba . . . Lyuba, he kept on saying her name, repeating it like an incantation, like a reminder of something hidden deep inside him, a riddle, a question posed without end. But even if he had gotten an answer, it wouldn't have made any difference.

4. Whimpering

A FEW YEARS have passed since that memorable night and the days afterward, when they took down the bricks covering over the door, and now Hooks sits on a bench, as far from the window as possible, and when he does peek, he just lightly darts an eye over the frost, because he's afraid he'll see blood. Blood falling from the clouds. And it's morning. Morning in the nuthouse.

It's morning, and noontime too rolls around without any fanfare, and Hooks shuffles his feet and narrows his eyes, and just once gives a little chuff, almost says something, when he runs into the doctor . . . finds somewhere to sit and doesn't talk, furtively studies his body parts, elbow here, knee there, a hand, doesn't perceive them as his, more like looking at a painting, and a pretty cold one too, but it's still better than lifting his head, because the sky . . . then he sits down to lunch and the orderlies set a plate of custard cakes in front of him, same as for most everyone else. Trade, a fierce voice whispers to Hooks from the outside world, trade, cunt! Hooks's plate is taken away, the owner of the voice sticks his plate in front of him, and Hooks stares at the mashed peas, stares because he's sitting under the window and doesn't want to lift his head . . . so he won't see the blood, maybe tears, he thinks, maybe through tears he wouldn't be able to see it so much. And he sits some more, squatting on a rear end jabbed full of injections, in his usual squatting spot by the toilets, and then it's visiting time and somebody gives Hooks a hug and lifts him up, a figure in leather, Brownie has come.

But Hooks, Hooks the Screw-up, says nothing. And Brownie comes again. And Hooks squints. And Brownie comes again.

With jams, smokes, and stuff. Even a dirty magazine. He knows
what comes in handy. But Hooks says nothing. Not out of
stubbornness, he's ashamed. He just can't. He stopped talking,
little by little, like this: he turned spee-ch-le-ss. But Brownie
talks. Including about Lyuba.

The crazies, who got used to Hooks like a new chair, and the
doctors, who keep their opinions to themselves, everyone walks
right past each other, jabbering away, just there somehow. They
let one out every now and then, bring in another. A couple head
cases, as if now that they'd lived to see winter they'd had enough,
kick the bucket. All they leave behind are their slippers and a
few odds and ends. The slippers get handed down, the rest goes
in the furnace. Half-naked she-demons stare out from magazine
covers, the kitchen cranks out the same old slop, madmen talk
on the radio. Some of the crazies started going for walks in the
garden. Single file. Hooks was spared that.

And then comes his glorious day, the day of déjà vu, and he
takes a hurtling toboggan ride back to his youth for an instant,
restoring his sight, his ability to take a steady, unclouded look,
and comes to terms with the bloody vision. In a fit of laughter
in the showers, he speaks.

Hooks didn't know they'd brought in King-size. He might
never even have noticed. But someone put a rag in his hand, so
he's wiping down the bathroom, some fat guy, new addition,
wallowing in the tub, washing up per local custom, eyes flashing
hungrily from underneath the showerhead. Hooks couldn't care
less, eyes don't scare him, not even the ones in his dreams. In
fact he's quite content, since the heavy steam is fogging up the
only window in there, so he knows he won't see the dangerous
clouds, he feels safely hidden, feels pretty good.

Hey, kid . . . comes a wheeze from the tub . . . hey, ever read
Sartre? The fat man rises up in the tub and Hooks straightens
up from his hunch too, rag in hand, and rasps out . . . Hey,
dumb fuck, wanna catch a fly? Heh heh, Hooks leers, and
something's going on with him, something's wrong with him,

and the fat man named King-size gets a bit panicky . . . Just tear off the wings, see, Hooks warbles in his nuthouse robe, an incredible grin on his face. And he looks! And he's got it back, all of a sudden he's in the outside world again, he smacks the well-read King-size in the face with his rag and speaks, suddenly he remembered his first time in the asylum and it brought him back from out there, where he was heading, slowly but surely, into apathy.

King-size drops back into the tub, keeping his distance. Guess I misread that psycho, an he ain't no kid no more either. He quickly rips out the showerhead, ready for a fight. But there's no need. Hooks is giggling, and he's still giggling in the nurse's office, he laughs all the way into the soothing straitjacket they slip, just to be safe, over the fine cloth of his nuthouse pants, the uniform, the one thing uniting the loonies.

Yeah, so when I saw him, Hooks told his friend Brownie, I suddenly remembered that sicko, remember? The one in Number Two with you.

Brownie nodded.

You met him, right? King-size?

I heard stories. So he's alive?

Oh yeah, Hooks nodded, as moved by the memory as an alumnus at a reunion . . . that jackass used to force little boys to . . . did he really get it from Sartre? He claims that's where he read it. You tear off the fly's wings, lie down in the bath so you've just got a little bit stickin out . . . the tip. Sounds bad, right? An you make the fly . . . what do you call it? March around? Pace?

Just forget it, said Brownie, don't even bother.

But you know, it snapped me out of it, said Hooks excitedly, some stuff's so sick it wakes you up, I got the giggles an snapped out of it, that numb state I was in, think it was the drugs? That whole thing. Man, I saw some . . . Hooks pulled up short.

But he could've gone on. Hooks could've gone on and on,

beside himself with happiness.

Hey, said Brownie, the character in leather, what's up with Lyuba?

Hooks turned somber. I'm a piece of shit, I know, he said. I was messed up.

You ditched, boy, you an Vera together, you were in Paris.

How do you know?

From Vera.

What? Hooks shot out of his seat.

Yeah, sit down, she's in town, here. Brownie handed him a sheet, a slip of paper.

That's her number. She's in Prague. Been back a while now.

She left, she ditched me, damn it, Hooks said to the air, gathering the nuthouse robe more tightly around him.

She says you ditched her. Says you left her back there. Says you guys invented something. Back there, in Paris. I know. An I'd like to know more.

Not me, said Hooks. I'd like to forget. Crossin that shit off for life.

We can talk about it when you get out, huh? Brownie said softly. Get psyched! he added.

Yeah, looks like a week from now, I'll be back in civvies, huh . . . walkin outta here.

What's up with Lyuba that you don't call or anything, Hooks's buddy asked with concern.

Listen, I gotta tell you . . . Brownie paused a moment, then leaned in toward Hooks. I've been seein a lot of Lyuba an she is strong, that is one strong lady. I had to tell you. About her an me. You been gone a long time. No letters, no nothin.

Hooks looked searchingly into the face of his friend in leather and the sky overhead didn't even bother him that much. But he blinked.

Nah, don't be stupid, c'mon, said Brownie. I'm just helpin her out, with the rent an stuff, y'know. We go half an half. She keeps askin about you, I keep givin her reports. Shit, you don't even call. Why'd you split? Like a dumbass. I can't even believe I'm tellin you. You gonna go back to her?

Yeah, I want to, I really do, Hooks said quickly, snuggling into his canvas tent. I just gotta wait a little . . . you know.

She's waitin, said Brownie, still waitin, you know her. He turned his attention to chewing his nuthouse apple.

And Hooks sobbed.

This is the day when a man is finally broken. When he walks across broken glass and rends his flesh with fiery thorns. When he covers himself in the rot and grime and filth of the universe, he must be a worm, he must pull the worms from under the threshold with his mouth, he must feel the pain, cut himself, beat himself. Assuming, that is, nobody else does it for him.

Brownie spat out the apple, reached into his pocket, and handed Hooks an orange.

Heh, Hooks sniffled, wiping the tears from his eyes, through which he had seen the light. Man, I hope that isn't . . . I hope it's not spiked with that crap.

I always thought you called it airfare, said Brownie.

I called it the ticket an I'm done. Those jams you brought, are they straight? An the smokes? I'm through with that, all of it.

Sorry, cool, no problem, said Brownie, broodingly taking a bite of the apple. He slipped the orange back in his pocket.

Wehh, whimpered Hooks. Wehhhhhh, he whimpered some more.

5. Lord of the Slab

MACHATA REACHED FOR the broom. Been a long time since he'd had some fun, and besides, the bitch deserved it. He'd had his eye on her awhile now.

When it was Helena minding the shop, not him, the Gypsy women would come in twos and threes, twittering and preening, showing all their colorful blouses, sweaters, and jeans to Helena till her eyes were practically popping out of their sockets. Meanwhile their hands were deftly slinking along the counter, stuffing cigarettes, lighters, pens, magazines, whatever they could grab, into their purses and under their skirts. Helena was staggered at how inexpensive their goods were, and in her incredible naïveté she heard out their sales pitch and haggled with them every single time. That was before. Now she wouldn't even give them the time of day. They never did sell her anything either.

Machata kicked the shop door shut, grabbed the broom, and battered the woman about the head, shoulders, back, as she hopped around, terrified, in the corner.

That'll teach you, you black slut, you thieving bitch, he panted. The woman cowered in the corner, shielding her face with her hands and screaming for mercy. Machata, built like a stack of bricks, was red in the face with the effort. He was enjoying himself. Still, eventually he got tired.

Outside it was getting dark, it was actually past closing time. Nobody else would be coming in now, he realized. But no sooner did the arousing thought flare in his mind—namely, to pin the skinny Gypsy bitch to the floor and give it to her good—than he dismissed it. He would've had to pull down the heavy metal security shutter and he should've thought of that sooner. Besides, even if he wasn't counting on any late shoppers, the Gypsy men might come looking for her. He wouldn't get off scot-free as it is, but roughing up a shoplifter's one thing, sticking your dick in her is another. And getting every Baiza and Grundza in the neighborhood on his tail. He grabbed her by the hair, stood her up, she looked dazed. But when he ran his paws over her breasts, she kneed him in the groin and ran out the door, he didn't even get a taste.

He tried to overcome the pain, his rage at the humiliation totally rattled his thoughts. Red and yellow spots swam before his eyes, not from the pain, but from the fury exploding inside him. He banged his fist down on the counter so hard he almost cracked it. Only moments ago he'd been afraid to try something with her. But now he would've welcomed it if the whole horde of neighborhood Gypsies had come to avenge her.

He'd had a fit like this once before, standing in front of a pub with a knife in his hand. But the guy he'd been waiting for had suddenly opened a window above him and dumped a trash can full of garbage over his head. The whole pub roared with laughter. Machata walked around the corner and plunged the blade into his thigh, had the scar to this day. It wasn't the only one on him.

Then he calmed back down. Before the sweat on him had dried. Surveyed his objects, his domain. I hit the jackpot, he told himself, havin the place an the shop together like this, I hit the jackpot, he told himself for the thousandth time now. Nadia was alone in the back, her puppy got tangled up in his legs. Outta the way, ya nutty mutt . . . his anger had passed now, and strangely enough, he actually kind of liked the pooch. What're you starin at, he snapped at Nadia, don't look at me that way, princess . . . he went to the fridge and, bending down, wondered if the girl had forgotten to put the beer in to chill again, his body stiffened with rage, but the bottles were there. Meanwhile Nadia cleared out of the flat, along with the dog.

Good thing too. Machata needed to think a few things over in peace and quiet.

He quite liked the new era. Business is men's work, women should sit at home, that was his favorite slogan. That was how he put it. He would've told it to the President or the Pope, the one Helena had a picture of over her bed. He would've shared it with the astronauts, just in case any distant worlds might care to hear his message. But right now Helena was his biggest concern. It looked like that religion stuff had messed her up in the head. He'd hoped by taking in Nadia it would lessen his wife's work, at home and in the shop, and she might come back down to earth. Nadia shouldered most of the work, she was good for that. Just like they trained her. It'd serve the girl well someday. But Helena was still like a stranger.

Machata took a sip of his beer and studied the bottle awhile. Helena either went out or spent all evening in the corner with her junk, straightening and arranging all her figurines and rugs. Either that or she prayed.

Not that Machata didn't tag one on Nadia every now and then, the girl could be slow to get moving sometimes. But today he'd seen those little bruises on her face again. Helena just wasn't herself. And who knew where she went, some meeting with the brothers, she'd said. If he ever caught her bangin one of those brothers, Machata snorted in amusement, that was one thing he couldn't picture.

She was a prayer, all right, his old lady. But there was something about her he loved. Her curtness, her straightforwardness. There was something about her he loved, something about her he needed, and he was angry she wasn't there now. They'd grown on each other over the years. He'd even gotten used to the new Helena. It didn't used to bother him when she got crocked from time to time. But then she'd changed for real.

At first he'd chewed her out. We went into private business together, damn it—pounding the table with his fist—an we're gonna stick it out together! Christ, it ain't easy. There's more important things, she'd said back, hissing through thin, clenched lips.

His respect for her had grown, he had to admit. He couldn't just lay into her like he used to. But oddly enough, he liked that. She gave off a kind of power, and if he, Machata, esteemed merchant Richard Machata, feared and respected on his home turf, had searched deep within himself, he probably would have found that he felt her incessant prayers somehow protected his little emporium, his wheelings and dealings. And some of his ventures were particularly in need of higher protection.

He strode around the flat, proudly taking in the heaps of brushes, boxes, and sacks, the foundation of his future wealth. Their place had been converted into a storeroom. Machata was building his business dung beetle–style. The time for a proper storeroom would come later. And it'll be equipped with a state-of-the-art security system, Machata daydreamed. For now he had to make do with what he had. And as for the storeroom . . . he had a plan. That evening he was going to see the lady who owned the building.

In the meantime, he had a thousand white "Alaska" brand candles stored in the bathtub. The closets were piled high with cans of paint. Eight "SuperBus" mountain-bike frames sparkled in the living room. Sacks of spices, dumpling mix, and crates of sardines stood neatly stacked around Machata's bed. The glass cabinet provided asylum to six hundred "Pulp" ketchup packets. And so on.

Machata was constantly rummaging through his property, acquired for the most part at sidewalk stands and street markets, counting and recounting, dusting off, puttering around the stacks. Today he also peeked in on Helena's room. The Pope wasn't up on the wall anymore, he noticed. The picture was gone. He couldn't have cared less about religion, the two of them didn't discuss it. Not since Helena had "converted," as she put it. Machata just accepted it. The same way he accepted the fact that Kučera's boy went to Sokol meetings now. It was all just part of the new era.

Machata wasn't a downtrodden super anymore either, an informer with a few juicy busts on his record, a small-time shopkeeper with a perpetual ax of debt hanging over his head. No sir, that was the old days. So Nellie prays, so what? What's it to you, pal? Other guys' wives were lying, drinking, whoring, lazy, money-hungry, clothes-crazy . . . Richard Machata, connoisseur of women, counted off on his fingers. And her taking down the picture . . . Machata was proud to have a Czech pope. Just like he was proud of Pilsner Urquell, Semtex, and Czech tennis players. Us Czechs're doin alright . . . besides, Vlk, sounds kind of warlike, manly. But the portrait was gone. Only the devil knew what Helena had in mind this time.

Machata went back to his beloved planning. The gradual conversion of the newsstand into a general store, that was his pride and joy. With his own hands, on weekends and in his spare time, he had knocked out a wall and put in a doorway so the shop and their flat were connected. It was pretty practical. Lucky for him it was no sweat making a deal with the landlord. Even luckier she was just a girl, didn't know shit about it, gave a guy some breathing room at least, he thought to himself happily.

Now that the door to the hallway was walled over, they entered the flat through the store. That way they didn't have to deal with the lowlifes in the building. Every night Machata pulled down the metal shutter, my home is my castle, he'd say to himself. It was a brand-new model twin-layer security grille, thing was like a drawbridge. He was the only one with a hook, had it custom-made. There in his castle, he had his wife, his girl, his dog, and his goods. Between them and the street was a massive slab of metal. Finally they could sleep in peace. Even the pup was trapped in there now.

Machata sensed more than heard that there was someone inside. In spite of his bearlike frame, he slipped agilely through the narrow hallway that led from the flat to the shop, snatching a crowbar off the table. He kept another one like it underneath the counter. Now he gripped it in his hand, prepared to use it on the late-calling customer, or be of service in whatever fashion might be appropriate. But he didn't have to exert himself.

What a pigsty, the latecomer muttered.

He crashed into crates, carts, the canisters and cans stacked all over the shop.

Lay off it, Machata told him, you'll be back, and gladly . . . I'm expanding, he couldn't help but boast. Knock down this here, he waved his hand, level out that there, he gestured, and then you'll see! I'll show you. I'll show alla you!

Yeah right, minimart. Dime a dozen! You seen the Australian's place? He was referring to the new shop, a modern convenience store a few blocks away. The place and its owner had already sucked close to a pint of Machata's blood.

Fuck you! Place is a scam, a bubble, it'll burst all on its own! You bring it?

What's this here? the late caller, a runt in a striped T-shirt and leather jacket, gave one of the canisters a kick.

Leave that alone, Machata warned him. Benzene. Wouldn't be stubbin my butt out on that, if I were you.

No shit? the little wise guy teased. He pulled out a match, in one fluid motion struck it against the stylish black denim that covered his scrawny lower half, and held the stick up to one of the canisters. His earring glittered in the flame.

You're an asshole, Machata snarled. The character blew out the match.

Take a look, said the guy, tossing a wad of bills on the counter.

Machata counted out the cash, nodded solemnly, then slipped two bills out of the stack and slid them across the counter. Joker didn't even move.

Aright, aright, the shopkeeper chuckled and added another two. Just testin is all.

How bout I deliver a few drops of this benzene here over to the Australian's place, whadda ya say? the character grinned, jokingly saluted, scooped up the cash, and tottered out.

Machata just stood there. That'd hit home. But he quickly calmed down. Not that a punk like that wouldn't plant the red rooster. And not that Machata wouldn't enjoy watching it flicker. But what about the guy then? He'd know. More than enough to squeeze him. Keep your distance, the wheeler-dealer said to himself.

He stepped outside, scanned the street, cars zooming by, stinking in the stench. He spit on the sidewalk, stretched deliciously, this was his turf. His eyes traveled along the street, sliding down toward the intersection, the sun was just beginning to set. Its rays played over the shutter, the massive slab of metal, it looked like a roasting grate now.

Machata spat in his hands and grasped the hook with gusto. As he pulled down the bars, they sliced though the sun's glare, metal biting into flame. My women'll just have to knock, thought Machata, master of the iron slab, least that'll teach em to come home on time. He thought about Helena and Nadia and the dog, came and went as they pleased, those girls of his. And when they showed up and knocked on the iron wall, Helena forcefully and somewhat angrily, Nadia softly and unevenly, he would gladly get up and go let them in. Right now he had work. Shunk, went the metal, and kcchh, it scraped against the sidewalk.

6. The Ticket, the Tunnel

Lyuba, yeah, Lyuba, Hooks intoned to himself . . . over and over, to the rhythm of the road, deep in the bowels of a dream where what had really happened couldn't have, he woke with a start.

He was sitting on a bus. Slowly, so as not to panic, he took in the unfamiliar buildings, the streets with foreign names. Vera's hand, warm and dry, rested in his. She was asleep, head on his shoulder. He blinked, shifted his gaze, peered into the gray light, it was morning. He saw a river. The bus came to a stop.

They got off with the other passengers, Vera staggering heavily, but still with a touch of grace. He caught her, caught hold of her, he really needed it. They were definitely in Paris, he recognized the steel frame of the Eiffel Tower. It seemed to be nodding across the river to them. Yep, it moved, it bent, he saw it. Blinked.

Well, check that one off the list, Vera said. Hooks stared. His girlfriend's head was shaved, red scratches, dried scabs, scattered across it, a random pattern of clumps of hair alternating with bald spots. He thought back to the night before. Had it really been only yesterday? He remembered holding her between his knees, by the neck, just in case, he'd said. So she couldn't change her mind. I want to be brand-new for you, she'd declared, there, in the bathroom. Well, she got what she asked for. He stifled a laugh, tried to recall if they'd brought any luggage. What's wrong? she asked, lifting her face to his. Ah, nothin.

Vera had come to him by way of Brownie. From him. He wasn't really sure. Brownie had introduced them. At the bar. She smelled boundlessly delicious. All over. It was insane, intense, and immediate. He broke out in a feverish sweat. Every time she looked at him that night. He fell off the barstool, almost broke his arm. Showing off. Bought some hash off Činča, chunks big as his thumbnail. Sparked it, that was the ticket. He urgently needed to drive the night into a frenzy, in every corner, at all hours. He knew what came next: graves parading before his eyes, people lying in them. He was gradually losing the past, the present was wounding him, and as for the future he didn't know shit. An uncomfortable time. Sparking up and inhaling wasn't enough.

He needed the ticket, needed something to drown out the hum of the fluorescent lights, the whir of the grindstone, the clang of the trams, the creak of wires in the wind and the gurgle of pipes underground, the siren, the buzz saw, fingernails on glass. The air shimmering with gasoline, the sky up above, and his brain wide awake: pain. His body was wholly defenseless. A very uncomfortable moment. So intensely uncomfortable he'd mistaken it for eternity. He didn't intend to stick it out.

He knew whoever takes a drug, himself becomes the drug. And either they stop or they're dead. He knew drugs had killed even among the first people. He knew drugs had come down to him through a chain of human bodies. Drugs circulate via bodies, live off the bodies of dead addicts. He knew it but left it for later. Right now he reached for the ticket.

He wanted to work magic, enter the tunnel, pass through it. And at the other end would be the inside of the girl's mouth, the interior map of her head, the rest he would toss aside, leave in the tunnel, he didn't need it.

He saw into her, right down to her toes, and let her see through all the false jungles of light into him, into the anthill of his mind. She sat alone, a neck, a head. He needed the ticket badly, to cover up the murderous noise. He couldn't stand even for a second the thought that any sounds might cause pain to that beautiful little thing. He would sooner have hurled himself from the ramparts. But the ticket was better.

He had to borrow some cash from Brownie. That was nothing unusual. Then they got hammered and got high. Together. Things got raw, but not for too long. When the old wounds laughed at them. They left them closed. Lay there, the two of them, looking at each other, looking forward. What a ride, she said.

He pictured her twenty-six or -seven years, or however much she thought he was dumb enough to believe, as a bouquet of red, white, and yellow roses, at its center a sweet tongue of timelessness wiggling. The image went to his head, and if the flowers had been in a vase he would've broken the glass and drunk up the water. He felt an urge to nourish them himself.

It wasn't at all like with Lyuba. Lyuba didn't use. If he'd been capable of reflection, he might have realized he'd grown so closely together with her that whatever he did, she did too. He lies here with the girl, Vera. Bent over her, doesn't lift his head. Doesn't look at the sky at all. There is no sky here. The tunnel.

But no doubt it was best to ditch Prague. So he cleared out of town. No: blew out.

Lyuba. Besides, he'd had enough of her complaints about his cooking. He only cooked for himself. Just enough for his trips into the tunnel. He needed them. Even Lyuba didn't realize how much.

And he absolutely never imagined how much his dubious art would appreciate in value here, with Vera in Paris, the city of poets.

A fine layer of hair was starting to cover her head again, how long've we been here anyway? he asked, scooping some crystals onto the tip of a knife.

The address of this tiny flat had also come from Brownie, who'd stayed here at one point. Their guest and household friend, Brownie's buddy Vladimir, fidgeted restlessly. Are we gonna get a move on, then? He was impatient to do business. The way these two were sailing, though, he could tell it was useless to try and torture their time with hours and days, strap their time to a rack they couldn't feel anyway.

Vera tended to be reticent, whenever Hooks focused acutely on her—as a human being, a female creature, or a spirit, not just as a less dependable part of himself—he got worried she was slipping away and he wouldn't be able to catch her. But he wasn't too concerned.

She wandered the streets for hours, he never knew where or if with someone else. Every so often they'd make up their minds to go back, but just the thought of buying tickets and figuring out the schedule was more than they could handle, let alone facing up to what they'd left behind, they each had their stuff . . . when they looked at each other it was obvious to both of them that one tense argument only led to the next and the next . . . another high, another run, another bed, from one rage to another, one promise to the next, next bottle, next day, next . . . whatever came in between.

Hooks had cottonmouth constantly, craved salt. He didn't eat much, and sometimes the drug made his tongue feel like rubber, so he'd sprinkle his little snacks, the occasional mouthful now and then, with huge doses of salt and pepper. Vera was more into sweets. On days when Hooks ventured out, he never failed to bring back a candy bar or two for his queen. At least to start with. Later on, he forgot more than just treats. He forgot her.

Vladimir was a sailor. But he didn't seem to care much how he made his living. He introduced them to the neighborhood, guiding them through the underpasses of Nurreille, uphill all the way.

There's a hun'red seventy-seven nationalities here, you'll fit right in, he'd assured them, as if they were worried.

In those days, back in '97, he had his connections on the Place de la République, all around it, in every block of flats, in the Chinese restaurants and game rooms around rue d'Aix and rue de Marlboro. He had his friends from the islands, most of them degenerates who, regardless of age, already had at least half their life behind them. He was on greeting terms with the nuclear engineers of the Secret Submarine Fleet, reacclimating from their claustrophobia in the city's covered passages. He knew the lighthouse moles and the brutal crews of the forecastles. He was friendly with the highest-priced seafaring pansies, blackmailers of officers' stripes. He'd learned something from each of them and owed something to them all. He could work a compass, forge banknotes, pick locks, even excelled at first aid. He lied constantly. He was flat broke. He was trapped. Like a gift heaven-sent to the two lovers from Prague.

Hooks's concoction quickly won the favor of the heroin skeletons from the arcades of Nurreille, with Vladimir making the intro. Is it good? Shit'd give your dog wings, Vladimir grinned at the junkies grasping for a rope, and raked in the francs. Vera was furious. Don't be stupid, she warned them, just for ourselves, we said.

Hey, Hooks reassured her, I know. But this'll cover our rent, our tickets back home, plus travel for Vladimir too, we can take him with us . . .

She was furious. She squirmed. But she accepted. She accepted a bump.

Mustafa and Ali, their next-door neighbors, dropped by to scout it out. Hooks didn't like the way they looked at Vera. Even if they did walk in arm in arm bearing flowers. But apparently all they were interested in was his cooking, his crystals. This isn't gonna work like this, we've got to get everyone on the salt! Vladimir advised him after the party.

Mustafa and Ali brought friends. Hooks would disappear into the kitchen, just snatching a lick here and there, hanging back with the flasks and alembics. Vera was the social one. She took charge of the up-and-coming salon. Swept the doorstep. Put the showerhead back in place after parties. Took out the trash and returned the bottles. Once, in a fit, scrubbed the floor. She began to check out the shop windows, came home with some gorgeous blouses. Stylish flats. A vest trimmed in gold coins. A cap with a pompon. Applied makeup to her lovely face in colorful, even layers.

Hooks, in a gray robe, skulked around the flat. Sat in the kitchen, building the crystal honeycomb, watching it grow. Ate her hallucinogenic pancakes. They rested their legs on each other and laughed. Tried out all the different ways they could put their hands on each other. She chased him around, he liked lifting her up. He spoke to her; she replied. She even learned how to imitate the muezzin. Stunned the Arab guests, all the junkies. Sometimes she'd just take a little taste and could handle conversation.

That was their life: Mustafa and Ali set up the hookah in the corner, the Moroccans brought the drums and rattles, Hooks tasted from the tip of the knife, Vladimir raked in the francs, and Vera in her pointy shoes stomped the excess salt into the table.

Others began to come too: Lebanese, Mauritanians, Cocker Spaniels . . . who could keep track . . . Vera passed around her pancakes. They made your skin crawl. The guests mumbled appreciatively. Vera served the crystals on a silver platter and Hooks's prestige grew in the eyes of their regular visitors while she became the pale goddess, the drug priestess, ever prepared for the graceful sidestep. They hung a Chinese lantern in the entryway.

Hasan served as Vera's personal bodyguard, accompanying her at a respectful distance whenever she went to the marketplace. One evening she came back with fish.

We're going to make a feast for our friends, Vera informed Hooks. Isn't it just wonderful having so many ebony friends? wiggling her ass at him, extending a leg clad in her new starburst stockings . . . her eyes swam, barely shining through from the other side of the drug . . . gutting the fish, she cut herself, sank to the floor. Hooks, standing paralyzed, nearly shed a tear seeing her there, on the ground in front of the sink, as if for the first time.

Hasan finished gutting the fish, clowning around with the bladder. Weaved through the kitchen smooth as a panther, glancing into pots, keeping a respectful distance from the alembics.

Girl, hey girl, Hooks slapping his love in the bathroom, hey, get it together, you're wasted, give it a break, you're was—smack from the left, ted—smack from the right. Hasan jumped on his back, almost snapped his filigree tribal necklace, they horsed around awhile.

Vladimir carried Vera down from the roof, she was about to fly away, propeller herself into the void, her naked arms cranking up, she was all ready to jump. By evening she was back at it again. With some local shaman, Nembo the lancer.

We don't have sex anymore, Vera said. We don't even try.

Hooks looked out at the storied rooftops like he was staring down a tube.

What're we doing here? he said. What're we hanging around for? This is bullshit.

Open that window back up!

Some buzz saw or something woke me up, said Hooks. As if she cared.

I was looking out the window, or no, wait, he thought a moment. First I screamed, I was screaming at the noise.

That's what woke me up, she said accusingly.

I thought I was in Prague, he said. With Lyuba.

Screw you, asshole.

An I shut the window.

Exactly, she said angrily, I'm lyin here all nice an cozy, takin in the fresh air, an you go an shut it! She got up, just in her panties, he noticed her breasts, mostly them, but he saw all of her, stomping toward him like a pint-sized general, eyes flashing rage, a bit sweaty with sleep, he was in awe, seeing her, suddenly standing at the window, his girlfriend, that crazy bitch, rearing up, a miracle of tenderness, standing on tiptoe, grabbing hold of the frame and yanking. It was like a pit to the outside, for him, stupid window. He almost fell out.

And they had an ugly fight.

I don't trust you anymore!

Good! You shouldn't!

What do you even feel for me?

What is that smell? Is that you?

Cunt!

Not yours, that's for sure!

A cunt like you isn't anyone's!

Next thing he knew he had hold of her, she slashed him across the face, he came back with a punch, hit her knife, tip of it scratched her, out came the red, she went berserk . . . kitchen stuff went flying, she gave him a shove, tea bags and canisters filled with rare spices, gifts to the pale priestess from her Arab friends, tumbled into his alembics, watch it, he shouted, shielding the stove with his body . . . then he was holding her, Vera, to his chest, suddenly the tension was gone and . . . with a sickening yearning he noticed her left breast, now, for the first time, it suddenly struck him as kind of . . . yeah, now of all times.

Bastard, she said, you are one sick fuck an it's only gonna get worse!

You . . . he said, you should talk, you're not gettin any younger!

What do you care, you're not my husband! she said, slipping out of the coffin.

I never knew that's what you wanted, he said, trying to steer into port.

I didn't either!

She tried to wipe the moistness from her eye so he wouldn't notice. He blew his nose.

It was awful. They felt awful. Early morning amid the scattered pillows. Major confusion. Too tired to lift an arm. How far can it go, they wondered, avoiding each other's eyes. But . . . then something happened. Later that day. By then they had covered each other in bandages.

7. Miracle in Nurreille

HE COULD TELL as soon as he took it. She sat next to him, they held hands. Watching each other. Infinite bliss. An incredible adventure, a demon-free flight. They stared at each other, wide-eyed.

Vladimir tried it too. He wasn't capable of words, but he raised the price. Mustafa and Ali hugged each other, sweating. There was no anxiety to disturb the effects. They were beside themselves. They were themselves. Vera smiled and a river of bliss ran through Hooks's heart, maybe an offspring of the drug, a previously unknown . . . compound.

This morning . . . I'm sorry, he told her.

Shhhh, she said. He laid his head on her chest. She could have chopped it off now if she wanted, bitten it off like a henbit, he couldn't move his neck consciously. But she took his head firmly in her hands and held it close. It was beyond love, beyond the insanity of love, and it was more than love. They knew each other. They had arrived at the end of the path.

That evening Hasan bowed down to Hooks and consumed the crystals from Vera's palm like the cave dogs of mythology. From that moment on, he maintained a respectful three steps away from the pale priestess. The other visitors were in ecstasy too. This drug, this new concoction, got everyone.

The white-haired man from Lebanon stayed at their place three days straight, dubbing Vera Imam of the Seven Blisses of the Tower of Men and Hooks the Blessing of the Entrails' Delight. Word got around the neighborhood fast. The mysterious Lebanese man left them the rug of rare fabric he had sat on the entire last day without blinking an eye; there wasn't a trace of human scent on it.

That same day Hasan's boys fended off an attack from the Georgians, and later that night the murky waters rolling through the gutters and catacombs of Nurreille washed up the dead body of Hedon, the dreaded loan shark. Amore Tapa, referred to by the local residents in fear and only in whispers as Shame of the Hill, leader of a terrorist group called the People's Fist, turned himself in to the authorities. Word on the streets was he did so at the pale priestess's request. Nembo the lancer addressed her that evening as Gazelle of the Plains, and he and his desert hyenas set up a round-the-clock watch over the flat.

Hand in hand Hooks and Vera walked along the knife-edge, the lip of the volcano, conducting exercises in coexistence in the mental gateway to the otherworld without even realizing it. The amazing concoction's reputation spread through the buildings and underground passageways of Nurreille like a fire across the steppes. The two lovers were drowning in cash, drowning in themselves.

How did it happen? Hooks wondered.

When we had that fight, Vera said. I love you.

In the kitchen? What was that about, anyway?

I don't know. I feel like I've known you a million years. When I threw you against the wall.

That stuff that fell off the counter. What was it?

They couldn't remember. But that had to be it. When they were wrestling, some of the spices, the teas, the drugs they'd received as gifts in return, some mandrake or something must've fallen in there, but which spice, which one? Hooks furrowed his brow. They had enough for now. Even Vladimir was getting high and blowing off business. At least he wasn't such a pain in the ass.

The door never stopped swinging. Vera received visitors while Hooks lived in the kitchen, experimenting feverishly. Nacha, pridol, wolfsbane, cnidaria, cat dander, none of it worked. He tried taxubulin, ferrous lactate, the curse of Zosia of Bulz, he crammed himself full of demon leaves and watched the bubbling mixture with a fiendish gaze, to no effect.

Vera peeked anxiously into the kitchen. Hooks sat in his gray robe, stuffing his face with ophiurida. It was one of the last things he hadn't tried yet. Love, she said. Ugh, he replied, eyes glued to the second hand. An alembic exploded.

In their spare time they basked in their popularity, strolling the streets, followers bowing down to them. Every derelict in the neighborhood grabbed hold of the ropes connecting them to the otherworld, swinging on them for all they were worth. Withdrawal was a thing of the past, a vague nightmare from the Middle Ages. The future was bliss. On the night of their conception the addicts' children would become other beings, human arks of altered genetic information.

Ever since the day Vladimir had bowed the messenger from the Sultanates out of the flat, there'd been no limit to the Eastern Threesome's fame. In honor of their invention, the Levantine Association of Nurreille declared the first day of the month of Jasper the Day of Bliss, marking the dawn of a new age. The bliss killed the pain. They all wanted it.

Wherever they went, Hooks, Vera, and Vladimir were surrounded by packs of little children and beggars holding out their hands. Followers and kindred spirits invited them into their homes, showering them with flowers and gifts. They lived in a cloud of music and adoration. Sorcerers bowed their heads, scamps whistled on their fingers, kettlesmiths banged their kettles. Even the ancient Jews of the Nurreille pits, hidden so deep in the catacombs that the thundering boots of the brutal invaders in WW2 were nothing more than the distant echo of a falling dove feather, surfaced from trapdoors in unexpected places, half covered in parchment as camouflage, to give Hooks knowing winks, haggle with Vladimir over staggering sums, and offer Vera giant raisins in recognition of her near-inhuman grace.

Vera's eyes were living fire, her body blazed with sex. She was the First Lady of Bliss. She began to be visited by dreams of the new age, and Rossana the All-Seeing herself sent a flock of her little brats to carry the train of Vera's dress.

Some of the derelicts began speaking in tongues. Leaving the Nurreille tunnel they went out into the city, and under the wild, dangerous sky they bore witness to the boundless delights of the new age of bliss. Others continued to come. A messenger from the town of Zirnj offered to grant Hooks a wish, and Hooks received a parrot. Plus a huge cage where the bird sat and talked. But I don't want him to talk to me, said the inventor, and a slave tore out the bird's tongue. But I don't want him to fly, Hooks stomped his foot. The slave melted the bird's feathers together with a blow dryer.

That's not what I meant, Hooks explained to Vera and Vladimir when he brought the parrot back to the flat. Mustafa and Ali were in ecstasy. Little Ali couldn't resist and pounced on Noh's feeder. Gaak, said the tongueless bird, giving Hooks a reproachful look, straight into his black junkie's heart.

But at night. At night sometimes it ate at him. That the concoction was running out. And he couldn't make any more. He couldn't figure out the missing ingredient. And then he saw it again. Vera was fast asleep, not a stir, he saw it on the pillow. The reflection. The red.

He screamed and sat bolt upright. She was sound asleep. Eyes open as usual. And he saw a red flash on the pillow in her line of unseeing sight. It was getting light. And the red skies, spread above the storied rooftops of Paris, closed in on him, and his vision of blood from the clouds came back. Drip, drop, drip . . . and gaak, Noh said to Hooks.

They didn't find him until almost an hour later. Are you crazy? Vera said. How'd you know? Vladimir asked. And: Why didn't you warn us, here, he handed Hooks a line with one end tied like a collar in a sophisticated sailor's knot around Noh's neck. They were standing in one of the Nurreille hill's underground passages.

What was I supposed to warn you of?

You know, that they were there, Vladimir said.

The police and the militia, Vera explained. They had the building surrounded!

What for? Hooks blinked, fingering his robe.

We barely made it out! Vera shrieked.

An we don't have a franc, Vladimir said. Not one damn sou!

They trudged up the hill. The sun wasn't out that morning. There was still a sharp bite to the air. The few pedestrians they met carefully avoided them. They noticed a curly-haired kid duck behind a lamppost, a dark-skinned child dip down a side street. The only one who didn't clear out of their way was a Chinese man in the underpass, who looked like he was watching them. That frightened Hooks.

They walked the streets. The shops and cafés were all closed. No smiling eyes or joyful energy. Gone was the jubilation, all the people who'd applauded them . . . gone. The miracle was over.

They were on their own, swung mercilessly by the pendulum to the other side of the otherworld. An addict's bloated corpse floated past in the canal below. Puppets nodded from windows. A mannequin in a display case offered Vera his swollen member in an unmistakable gesture; the worms were already at work on him. His eyes were watching Hooks too, he ran a finger across his neck. Vladimir didn't notice, standing rigidly listening to a rat that said it was going to kill him. The stink in the air was unbearable. Like the anxiety in the building next door had just thrown on a change of clothes, glanced at its festering watch, and dashed out for a date with death. Gaak, said Noh. They'd hit bottom, hard.

He went back to Lyuba. After a couple weeks. After all they'd been through. After they'd broken up. They left Noh with Vladimir. But they couldn't go on together.

You're goin . . . you're goin back to her, aren't you, she said.

We can't help each other, he said. We can't help each other anymore. You an me.

But we can't leave each other either, she said.

No, we can't. You stayin?

Maybe, whatever. I'll be alright.

She must have stayed, since he kept spotting her. At least he thought he did. In the metro, through a shop window. A few times in the bar where he worked. He said something. She pretended not to understand. But probably he was wrong. It probably wasn't her.

He thought back to the first time he'd seen the red flashes here in this foreign city. They'd come at him while she was asleep, out of her unseeing eyes. And merged with the red in the sky. He thought about her, but the image in his mind was tattered, soaking wet from the constant drip, drop . . . what Hooks saw falling down from the sky.

8. The Pit

SOMEHOW HE GOT there. Standing again at the Angel Exit inter-section, and now he saw the pit too, people were disappearing into it. Not everyone, he saw a young woman with a baby car-riage, she walked around it. He saw a dog who dug in his claws, wouldn't go any farther. Even when they tugged him by the collar. He met an old man who he was sure could also see the pit.

He watched the blood, falling down from the clouds. He stood there and saw people vanishing into the pit. He heard snatches of conversation, voices. In every face, he knew them from his dreams, in every wrinkle, in people's skin and in every moment of that skin now he saw only pain like a disfigurement, somehow they were giving it to him. He took it, without knowing why. I'm obsessed, he thought. A tremble shook his body. And maybe for a minute he regretted not being gifted with the power to exterminate those people. It would probably have been better for him to stand on the edge of the crater alone.

He saw the red sky over Angel, shredded by incoming clouds coiled in on themselves.

He saw the dark sky over Angel, watched the pulsing veins of neon light, which grew together to form the tissue of darkness, coming in from every direction. He walked the streets, home again, avoided people and bumped into them, he was at home here, among his own.

the sky tears open
and among the red sails

you see a body
maybe it's somebody's chest
pierced through and you feel
the hatred of the world within you
and you know:
everyone here will be dead
and your hatred and your horror
are strong are so powerful
they want to explode
and tear you apart:
the day it happens
everything you ever ate
will cook again inside you

He couldn't tear himself away from the intersection just yet, went to eat some chicken. On the snack bar counter a rose glittered like a little plastic heart, there was water in the vase, kind of moldy, they kept the salt in see-through glass. They sold the chicken in quarters, meat sizzling as it turned on the spit, Hooks pointed to the one he wanted, they sold the pieces wrapped in silver paper. Then he tried a beer. A coffee. Walked back out.

He discovered a McDonald's had opened while he was away, across the street from the synagogue. Someone had pinned a note to the synagogue's beat-up door: "I was here again. Herschel. 1942–1997."

Grown-ups and kids sat in the McDonald's, someone talking into a mobile phone, someone just casually tying his shoes. Hooks walked past the mirrors, trying to get used to it. Surprisingly nobody screamed at him: You've got blood in your hair and on your jacket! What are you doing in here?

He walked all day long, all evening, walking around the pit, and saw the Ukrainian gang, headed up by Vaska the Tyrant and Killer Kolya, swarming down the street. Hooks graciously stepped aside, avoiding Number Six. Dog Six had also just come home, they gave him a buzz cut as a parting gift, so he'd run a razor over his skull from the nape of his neck to his forehead, the stripe looked pretty bizarre but he felt like he stuck out less. Next, Hooks dodged an encounter with Bent Devil, who picked out his prey from the rooftops and went straight for the jugular, and without even realizing it he also ducked out of view from Yellow Plague, who'd just tied on his sneakers down in hell and headed up top for a while . . . Old Yellow liked living in bodies, their coexistence often began as a sensation of cold in the bones, people called it cancer.

Then Hooks avoided a pack of genetically modified forest spirits, they'd been hired to dig up the asphalt at the intersection, the project was supported with generous grants from the state in a joint venture with the underworld, but they came there for the phenol; all they had left were holes where their nostrils used to be, hobbling along on their stumps, swiping a shopping bag or two, beating up senior citizens . . . he steered a wide path around the pit where the people were disappearing, scared he might see Lyuba in there and scared to go where he had to.

Then he walked through the park planted with little trees, by the church, and a Roma gang was playing soccer with a head snatched from a cab, and the Czechs sat in their cars, tuning in to their favorite stations. And the sky was red. He kept walking, almost all the way to the building where she lived, but he didn't go in.

He saw the red sky and watched. Took from people what they gave him, and there was a lot of fear and filth in their pain. He went back to the pit and loitered around the intersection. And the sky was red. He knew he had to find . . . something within himself, down by the bottom, in the depths gaping like the chasm of the pit. He reached inside himself, within, sidestepping the crush of the streets, the people. He knew he had to find something. Otherwise he was done. He waved down a car.

And maybe it started to rain, because he definitely had moisture in his eyes, maybe that was what flipped the switch.

When the cab stopped for him, Hooks saw his neighbor, the shopkeeper, pulling the grille down across the storefront. And oddly enough, at that exact moment, a couple seriously red sunbeams reflected off the grille and boom: Hooks's eyes were full of them.

Uh-uh, we're goin to Bohnice, he told the cab driver.

What?

Bohnice, please, the mental hospital, Hooks said out of the corner of his mouth. A grimace had spread across his face. And hard as he tried, he just couldn't stop it.

As you like, said the driver, taking a closer look at his fare. But, ahem, if I may be so bold, I assume this isn't for a visit? At this time of day?

No, it's not for a visit, said Hooks. And to reassure his deliverer he showed him his cash. Enough for a one-way trip.

9. Nadia

NADIA SLIPPED PAST the woman with the bag and stood in the back of the tram. Mook, who up until then had been lying limply in her arms, just wheezing in and out, suddenly reared up. It took all her strength to hold him back. He bared his fangs, coated in saliva, then collapsed back into her arms. Huddled up in the blanket, only his head peeking out. Where you going with him, the woman asked, is he sick?

Nadia panicked at the woman's mention of sickness. She would never make it to the doctor's on foot if they threw her off the tram. Luckily there wasn't anyone else in the back to hear. She felt Mook stiffen, muscles straining, front legs poking her chest.

The tram kept stopping so much, Nadia was afraid the doctor's would close before they could get there. She was hoping they'd give him a shot or some pills. They wouldn't let him die, would they? He even breathing still? the woman asked. He was having convulsions. I don't mean to give advice, child, but you might be wasting your time.

Up until now Nadia had been able to feel the dog's heart beating against her chest, even through her coat and the blanket, but all of a sudden he just felt cold. His eyes were cloudy, but they'd been like that before. A membrane had covered over his eyes, his body suddenly heavy, still.

Well, if you're going to the vet's, I'm sure they can tell you, the woman said, and turned away.

Nadia turned to face the window so the other passengers couldn't see Mook. Anyone looking now might have thought she was holding a doll in her arms.

She tried to just concentrate on the route. There's a turn coming up, then one more stop, then the one after that, she said to herself. She couldn't imagine Mook being dead, not being there anymore.

They used to live out in the country. It was Mook who'd found her, not the other way around. That was back when he was still tiny. The old lady said to give him some milk. The old lady had called him "pooch."

Her arms hurt but she held him tight. Mook looked weird with his yellow eyes, teeth clenched, they looked scary. It reminded her of werewolves. The old lady had shown her a werewolf one night. It looked like a big black dog. Then they had fled home, running across the fields, barely able to catch their breath. The werewolf sniffed around their house, ready to eat them up.

The old lady told her werewolves were people who turned into savage beasts at night, they killed their victims and sucked their blood. In the morning they changed back and walked around the village like everything was normal. Nobody ever recognized them. From then on, Nadia had kept a close watch on her neighbors. Remember, the old lady told her, they've got the devil's lamps in their eyes.

The old lady taught her to protect herself by tying blades of grass to her clothing and wearing knots under her dress. She taught her when to cross her fingers and which prayers to say fast in her head. Nadia knew what to do if she ever got scared, in the woods or in the house. If she was ever alone.

The old lady taught her to make a doll and explained how it worked. She showed her how to make the figure and what to say when she stabbed it. She could do it with a splinter or a needle. But she could only do it once, she said. She said she was teaching Nadia because she was little. Because she was little and different from everyone else. The old lady promised Nadia that she would never leave her.

One night, when Mook was still a puppy, the old lady died.
Nadia could tell right away. Her face turned yellow and pointy.
Mook started whimpering, that was the first time she took him
to bed with her. He didn't want to lie next to the old lady, so she
put him on the other side, he kept her back warm.

In the morning Nadia noticed the gas burner was on. The
flame was on high, she could feel the heat. She must've forgotten
to turn it off the night before. She lowered the flame and put on
a big pot of water. She had to use two hands. She knew what to
do, the old lady had told her plenty of times. First she washed
her, then she took a clean dress out of the chest.

The woman who came for Nadia hit her when she tried to
tell the old lady good-bye. The woman was in a hurry. At least
she let her take Mook. As they were leaving and the woman was
locking up, they heard a noise from inside the house. Nadia
knew who it was and she knew they wanted out. The woman
dragged her away by the hand, but Nadia crossed her fingers
and said the words to herself.

The woman got drunk at the train station bar and Nadia
started to cramp her style. You can keep her, she yelled to the
guys at the tap. One of them took Nadia on his lap and said he'd
be glad to take her home. Nadia hoped he'd let her take Mook
with them too. The man said he had a dollhouse, he just needed
a doll. But after a while he forgot and let Nadia go. Somehow
they made it onto the train and the woman fell asleep. They
rode a long time.

If any of the passengers now, on the tram, had looked at
Nadia from the back, they probably would have thought she
was holding a doll in her arms, or maybe some big rubber toy.
If their vision had been sharp, they might have seen through
her ragged coat, sweater, and T-shirt to her skinny back covered
in cuts and bruises, the old ones slowly taking on the color of
meat, and the fresh ones, yellow and blue, keepsakes of blows
with a hand, a shoe, a chair, whatever happened to be within
reach.

The woman hit Nadia often, sometimes to punish her, sometimes just because. The man hit her less and never in the face. Nadia never knew when they would hit her and when they wouldn't.

Two or three times the man came to Nadia in the night, took his penis out of his pants, and tried to stick it in her mouth. Three times. Nadia tossed her head side to side, dodging the thing dangling in front of her face, sometimes she hid under the quilt and he would leave her alone. But she had to go to him when the woman ordered her to. Otherwise she'd get a beating. Sometimes the woman beat her anyway.

Then the woman changed. She wasn't around so often. She stopped yelling at Nadia. She didn't walk around drunk and bring strangers back to the flat anymore.

Now she just sat on her bed, doing nothing for hours but moving her lips. Sometimes she would rearrange the things on top of the bureau. Pictures, statuettes, medallions, she brought all kinds of things home these days. Sometimes Nadia looked at them, but she never touched. She knew the woman would be able to tell.

She also didn't send Nadia out to look for the man anymore. He worked in the flat now, he was there all the time. Sometimes Nadia would help him, holding the measuring tape, bringing him nails. Boxes and bags filled the flat. One whole wall of the bathroom was covered with cans. Nadia wasn't strong enough to carry them, but she could at least arrange the paintbrushes by size. They formed a chain and loaded the bathtub with candles. Knocked out a wall.

Nadia used to have to go and fetch the man, making the rounds of the neighborhood pubs with Mook until they found him. Usually he spotted her peering around the room from the tap, bought her a soda pop, and walked home with her when she was done. Sometimes he reached under her dress and fondled her along the way. But often he was so drunk he could barely walk. He didn't say a word. They also used to send her to the pub for beer. One day the door slammed shut and they had to wait, so the woman gave Nadia a key, which she wore around her neck.

Now the woman wasn't there. Only Nadia knew why. She had molded a figure out of wax from a candle she stole. That night, standing over the figurine as it writhed in pain, its little face contorting as she ran the needle through it, Nadia spoke. She said it out loud. And she got an answer.

She decided to do it after the woman swore she was going to poison Mook. She told the man she'd do it too. The night before, the woman had swept the statuettes off the bureau, screaming and shouting. Rolling around on the ground. They couldn't hold onto her. She said bad words, nonsense. Spat on the man. Scratched up Nadia's face and kicked Mook. All he did was snap at her once. The woman's leg started to bleed. She said she was going to leave them. Wouldn't stop screaming. Then the man hit Nadia, kicked Mook too. He looked around the flat for the woman. Then went out to look for her. Now he was waiting for her.

Nadia thought he would be glad when the woman went away. She thought now she would be his wife. She started to think that after they walled up the doorway together. Now every night she knocked on the grille and the man came and opened it. Yanked it up with the hook, just enough for her and Mook to squeeze underneath. He never got mad at her. He knew the dog had to go out at night.

Nadia thought it didn't bother the man that she was mute. That she didn't talk to him. She wanted them to be together. The woman had been so mean to him. Why should he care if she came home? Nadia had learned to cook a long time ago, and she and the man often ate alone. There was always enough left over for Mook. She thought they would go on living like that.

But now she didn't have Mook anymore. The woman had somehow managed to do it to him anyway. From wherever it was she was now.

It was raining. The rain was cold but light. Nadia barely noticed. She was sitting on a bench in the park. Under a lamp that suddenly came on, and Nadia saw a face. A statue, or what was left of it. It had been hidden in shadow, covered up by the bushes. Nadia shifted and saw it. It was terrifying.

Maybe it was a ghost. She remembered how the doctors had thrown Mook into the oven. They didn't even try to make him better. They just burned him. They took the blanket she'd wrapped him in so he wouldn't catch cold on the tram and handed it back to Nadia. Here, take it, they said. She ran away and left it there.

Now she sat looking at the ghost right in front of her. Little white pieces of paper were stuck on the branches around it, moving. The bush was alive, moving in the wind, the pieces of paper looked like teeth. Like a mouth, ready to gobble her up. She closed her eyes and opened them again. Crossed her fingers.

The ghost didn't move. Somewhere high up above she heard a bird squawk. She heard the wind. A couple leaves dropped from the tree above her head. It was dark out. Nadia got up and walked out of the park. Went back to the street, to the flat, the grille. She had no place else to go.

10. Welcome

THEY HAD LET him out, why not. They were probably glad to be rid of him. It wasn't a particularly heartfelt good-bye, they were afraid they'd get stuck with him again. Eventually.

But Hooks had made up his mind. To live with it. Somehow. Anyway, according to the simple philosophy of the tame crazies, everyone's got a deficit in one area and a surplus in another. Balance is impossible.

And whenever Hooks compared his red hallucination to the delusions of some of the veteran schizoid psychopaths . . . the sniveling creatures slogging through the fetid, oozing swamps of endogenous depression, the sorry wrecks of human beings, flies caught in the voracious web of paranoid schizophrenia, when the spider that sucks you painfully dry is your very own brain . . . amid those mountains of insanity, in that desert of terror, a sky red with blood was practically like winning big in the lottery.

An I mean we're all playing the odds, right, Hooks thought as he left the booby hatch, stepping out again in his civvies, back to try his luck in the lottery one more time. Drip, drop . . . and besides he'd realized, heh-heh . . . this is no hallucination, Doctor, this is no whatchamacallit . . . psychagogic pseudohallucination caused by drugs and a dissolute lifestyle, this is for real. Blood just falls sometimes. Out of the clouds. The sky is red. Some see it, some don't.

And so: back on the tram, around the intersection and through the intersection, Angel, with its man-eating pit, gaping wide to welcome those who vanished into it.

He got off the tram. And started walking. Crisscross, back and forth. Testing the cobblestones, stomping the ground. He confronted the evening time Angel, cast in the dreary glow of an ordinary intersection. He was back again from somewhere else. Back again at the intersection. As ordinary as they come, the kind civilization spews out like a copy machine: trams, buses, cars, moms and bums, crowds back and forth, in and out of the subway, winos and screaming tots, established residents, gypsies, chinks, beggars and spooks, baby carriages with brand-new participants, smog. Above it all.

He saw the red sky, tried to get used to it . . . cunningly accept it as fact. He saw it and attempted a bored yawn, even though his unprotected nerves were practically boiling . . . he could feel them, under the weight of the sky, fracturing like split ends craving a curling iron, a burning touch, to give them shape . . . his heart pump howled to a strange rhythm.

He knew it was there. And knew he had to do something about it. Himself. He had to find an antidote. It was up to him, it was in him.

He decided to ride through the curtain falling from the clouds. He survived, made it through.

And just to make it double clear to the powers of the otherworld, he got off, hopped a tram going in the opposite direction, and rode through Angel Exit one more time. He even looked out the window. Raising his pain threshold. He could go all the way down to the bottom and still bounce back. He was home again, on the filthy street.

Gripping the bar tightly, he stared out past a couple fashionable hats and artful perms, right into the trolleys, the wires, the soot, the blood. And then did it again. And again. And it was okay. His tram pass was permanent too.

Welcome, she said. As soon as she opened the door. C'mon in. I've been expecting you.

He went in. Expecting?

Yeah. Expecting you to show up. Want to stay?

Yeah.

For how long? she said.

For good.

Ha, she said. Ha-ha.

And then he said: Welcome to hell. Ladies first. Like always, like usual. Like in real life. He finished his recitation and stood gawking at her.

She looked pretty good. Almost the way he remembered. Her hair was in a bun, held in place by a barrette. The heavy one. The one she'd had the first time. He took it as a sign.

Amazing. You made that up? A little present, huh? They give you a lot of pills? I hope they gave you the treatment.

Oh yeah, lots, I didn't always take em.

So you thought you'd get away with it?

No. I don't know. I didn't think.

I know. You really think you can live like this? With no rules?

Mm, uh, he said. They were still standing there, by the door. He could have pulled it shut and been gone, but if he slammed it now, it would stay closed forever. He knew that. He didn't want that.

The rules are set. Everyone knows them. Anything else I need to add? Perhaps concerning our situation, our, shall we say, relationship?

No need. Got any cigarettes?

I don't smoke.

No? Hey, wow!

He suddenly noticed the flat was different. Stunning new furniture. Big table. He stood in the room that used to be his before they knocked out the wall. There was a new door, he opened it and walked into the next room. Then through another door to another room. Curtains, TV, flowers, like a castle. He turned to her.

That's right, I got the buildings back. It's mine. Still a lot of paperwork to deal with.

I noticed they tore down the balconies. People come in through the building.

I'm surprised you didn't get lost.

So it's yours now?

Ours, if we get married.

Huh?

You heard right. I can say it again if you want. I made risotto. You hungry?

What about you?

I already ate.

He needed a drink. Eating rice is almost impossible with a dry throat. Even in spite of the hunger, the hunger of the alien creature, the mangy little demon inside you who so happily rips your guts out, forcing you to hunch, huddle, almost not exist. She drank too. They left the bottle out on the table. They had plenty to talk about. And it got better by the minute.

Kind of like a ship on a stormy sea, and despite the snapped lines, lightning striking the mast, a decimated crew, and rats running wild below decks, it finally sails into the cove. The survivors explore the coast: Will a pack of cannibals come swarming out of the jungle, or some peacefully inclined, fascinating people draped in flowers? Will there be drinking water, or stagnant sludge? Friendly creatures, or saber-toothed tigers? They explore it. They explore themselves, and it's fine. In spite of it all. And what with everything. But they know the voyage is not over yet. Not as long as they're alive.

Hooks and Lyuba drank. True, when she got a buzz on, he got a bit of an ass-kicking. But he was glad. Even if the dishes, and whatever else she was able to get her hands on at the moment, hurt. At least he knew for sure it was real. He had no idea they made so many kitchen appliances. Some of them were brand-new. Now he got a good look at them. But she wasn't out to kill him. Definitely not. That wasn't how she would've done it.

She was resolved. She had waited and here he was. They had

the street on one side, the courtyard on the other. Farther away there were hills sprinkled with winding lanes, built of cement, bricks, concrete. There were condemned ruins and demolitions. Wild grass, freezing underground, shot up through cracks in the sidewalks. Crows perched on black tree branches, watching. Garden walls were topped with crushed-up beer bottles. A self-important German shepherd stood guard here and there. Some things went on in buildings, some in the cellars underneath.

They lived here, this was their turf. They breathed the pale air wafting through the lanes on the hills. Lyuba was resolved, she had her rules, he fit into them.

Before they went to bed they got stoned. But just a little. Then Lyuba Love cleared the dishes and Hooks the Visionary dozed off in his chair. Suddenly he was dead tired.

Heh-heh, Brownie grinned. And: Ho-ho, he gave Hooks a manly slap on the back. Hooks got an unexpected urge to clock his buddy one. He was a little taken aback at how well his friend knew the place. Oh, c'mon, it's just for a while, Lyuba said. Just till today! Brownie specified.

He was using one of the rooms in the flat for storage. It was Hooks's least favorite, the one Lyuba used to live in, before him, walled in, with the window on the courtyard. How many times had Hooks vowed that he'd put bars on there.

There were so many rooms in the flat that Hooks the Psychopath and his bride-to-be, Lyuba Love, were going to share together. Too many, he thought.

He wandered. Tripped over the rugs.

If it'd been up to him, he would've swept Brownie and his religious trinkets right out the door.

Try to understand, said Brownie, where else was I gonna put it. He knocked on a crate filled with copies of *Closer to God*.

Check these out, they're hilarious, he said, handing Hooks a comic book on living the Christian life. He had boxes of them. Pounds. In full color. He had Nativity scenes. Wind-up Bibles.

A smiling Jesus with Roman soldiers and the apostles. Assorted Virgin Marys.

Unbelievable, said Hooks. Total crap.

Oh yeah, I know, said Brownie. Like I said, it's temporary. Just a little sect like.

Why would you want to go an get involved with maniacs? Hooks said to Lyuba. She was holding a plastic facsimile of St. Engelbert's lance.

I already am involved with one.

Ho-ho, Brownie said. Plus there was plenty of room here, if you get my drift. Since you weren't here.

So there's money in this? asked Hooks.

You'd be amazed, said Brownie. I'm the group's central distributor. But I already got something else scoped out. A gold mine! I'll tell you about it tonight. Hey, there he is. You gotta see this!

Hooks looked out the window. A handcart wheeled into the courtyard. Then a head came into view. The head and shoulders of a big man. Hooks almost flinched. The guy had a scar across his face, thick black eyebrows, longish hair. There was no way Hooks could know that he had let his mane grow to cover the scars of his sliced-off ears. And if by some chance he had been able to catch a glimpse of the unsightly stumps through his hair, it wouldn't have been an uplifting sight. The man looked to be around fifty. Lifted his head and looked at them. It made Hooks mad that he could see Lyuba. It made him mad he hadn't put those bars on the window.

The man's voice, though, was surprisingly soft . . . kind . . . that was the word that came to Hooks's mind.

Greetings, brothers. And to you, sister, he said. Standing, looking at them. Watch yourself, Brownie whispered to Hooks, and squawked: Greetings, brother Lurya!

Greetings, brother Lurya, the man echoed back.

To work, brother Lurya, Brownie said. He smirked at Hooks and tossed down a package of books to the man.

The man went into motion and they formed a chain, passing the books and the rest down the line. The man caught the things in flight sure-handedly, smooth and easy, just rotating his trunk. His hands were like shovels. Like weapons.

A car in these little streets, Brownie said, it's ridiculous. A mule's what you need! An that's what he is! You're a mule, brother Lurya, isn't that right?

Yes, I'm a mule, brother Lurya, said the man. I'm whatever the Lord would have me be.

Brownie was poking fun at the guy. Hooks didn't like it. Leave him alone, he said . . . he could squash you like a bug.

He can't, said Brownie, he's a believer.

Why does he call you that weird name? asked Hooks.

That's what they all call each other, said Brownie. He went downstairs to the courtyard and took some cash from the man. Quite a bundle. Quite a few thousand. Lyuba declined when Brownie tried to give her a "little something," a storage fee, as he professionally put it.

The man came several times that day. Each time he handed over a wad of cash to Brownie. By evening the room was empty. Except for a single orange Nativity scene that Hooks had burned for heat. But he wouldn't let Brownie push any money on him.

What're you gonna do with all that cash, he asked his buddy when they finally sat down.

What else? I'll tell em: Later, fanatics!

We wouldn't want any devil's parishioners breathin down our necks, said Hooks.

You been readin too many magazines, don't worry, I'll handle it.

Are they Jehovahs or what? You sure they're not Satanists? That guy is weird, him an that cart of his. I was glad when he left. Everyone on the block was freaked out. I'm surprised Lyuba let you.

Well you know, said Brownie, she was broke till they gave her the buildings. I helped her out. She was payin rent! Forget everyone on the block. She was down. Rock bottom, get it? You need to know that. Don't go judging her.

Why would I? I'm just glad she didn't kick me out. It's a miracle.

She's amazing, said Brownie.

I know. Hooks didn't feel the need to go into it.

Thanks for helpin her. Yeah, I flipped. Should've been takin care of her.

What happened, happened, Brownie said, stuffing his leather pockets with cash. We're just glad to have you. Lyuba an me. An everyone else. Take a walk up the hill? Come to the pub, first round on me.

I'm pretty beat.

You been lyin around a long time. Don't want to overdo it, before the wedding.

How do you know? Hooks bristled.

I just figured, his pal Brownie said. D'you call Vera? he asked quietly and quickly. Shh! Hooks hissed. Hey, Lyuba, you coming with? Hooks called into the next room. He yelled loudly, but there was no need. When he turned around he saw that Lyuba was standing in the doorway.

No, she said. And be back soon. Just be back, she joked.

11. Bliss

FAITH, HOPE, AN love. Said Brownie. Faith, hope, an love, boy. I'm talkin capital letters. That's what people need, yep, an some need it in pictures an signed by the Pope. That's where I come in, check it out. He spelled out a word in the sparse cover of snow. Drew it with the steel-plated toe of his boot.

Vlk, Hooks read out loud . . . yeah, so?

You don't even know they elected a Czech. You really have been gone a long time. An not exactly hangin around churches, I realize.

So you traffic in religious stuff, said Hooks. But you didn't convert. You're the same. Not only that, but I think you want to take their money. The whole thing stinks.

Maybe I need to get rich to help humanity! What do you know? Converted, not converted, Brownie flashed a grin, same difference. Bottom line's simple. The rules are set. Faith, hope, an love, I give you these three words! It's about bliss. People livin in peace. Heh, you'll see . . .

Gimme a break, said Hooks. They climbed the hill. Walked through the park. It felt good breathing in. Breathing out. Moving.

There were trees.

He opened the pub door with the old familiar grip. All his friends were there. Sitting at the same table. Brownie had set up a welcome-back party. Hooks sat down, touched for a moment as he took in the faces through the wisps of smoke.

Some were the ones that surfaced in the red twilight of his dreams, he knew the blood that flowed from the clouds was their blood too, it too had dug the pit.

Maybe it works the same as photosynthesis, he thought in a quieter moment, once they had dispensed with the opening ceremony and the conversation swerved back into the usual shortcuts and anecdotes.

Yeah, he said to himself . . . it comes from people's insides, it soaks into the clouds an then falls back down. That's it. He was sure he'd see the clouds again, traveling across the sky, drunk on blood as ticks.

The pub on the hill was like a living museum of communism. In fact no, even further back, there was nothing superfluous here, nothing to distract the cavemen from their fire. No modern-day comforts. An ad or two, for appearance's sake. Couple video slot machines. It was like the locals here had steeled themselves against the flow of time. Their internal and external worlds were more in synch here than in some wannabe Eurobar blasting robotic music. From one of the walls a blonde pinup gazed down on the drunks with a cruel, knowing smile. A true lady. She had been hanging there in the frame for as long as anyone could remember, nobody knew her name. It was enough decoration for everyone there. It was more than just a decoration.

Apart from that, fluorescent lights and Formica. The grime and scars on the walls scared off any aesthetes. The patrons here discussed literature and philosophy up till age seventeen or so. Anyone who still had a thirst for knowledge after that went elsewhere to quench it. Here they played dice and read tabloids. Because sometimes you just have to put up with life. This was a place where you could lie low. Their sour beer was the cheapest in Prague. Which explained why they had some shady callers every now and then. It wasn't for nothing the guys at the tap were called Paratrooper and Cap. Compared to the days when the cops raided the place with dogs, dragged the boys and girls away, and sat them down under their own, much brighter lights, the occasional incursions of drunks just livened things up a bit.

Instead of petitions being passed around under the tables, now it was drugs. Nobody saw society as a monster anymore, now it was about fending off the monster in yourself. Sometimes by howling. There was nothing waiting for you at home except walls, and maybe the person you lived with. A scary movie on TV, there was always that. In the morning you might wake up here or someplace else, alone or with someone. Then it went back to being just you. But that moment could be postponed. This was one of the places to do it.

Once upon a time, the youngbloods of the underground had cut their teeth here; today young people were taking the measurements of their caskets for themselves. The former denizens of the underground who latched onto politics or wrote for culture sections just stopped in for a round or two every now and then, for old times' sake. Hunched over the Formica with the ones who'd stayed behind, they could see more clearly how high they'd climbed.

The former allies from the psych wards, lockups, and protests traded phrases back and forth, drug dealers with ministers' advisers, each testing out their own newspeak. They'd all had their world fall apart; they each had to rebuild it somewhere else. And the underground, playing its classic offstage role, returned to one of its oldest haunts and turned into the underworld.

In summer, fires flickered in the trash cans outside. Wax evaporating from paper cups. Syringes broiling, giving off a plastic stench. The flames dark blue, sometimes purple. You could watch the sun as it set. A dwindling blaze, an unknown planet. You could see the trees turn dark. The chairs were attached to the outdoor tables with rusty chains. When you stepped on a tube of pills or a glass syringe, it crunched under your shoe like sand.

Hooks had his first cautious beer. A few people came to say hello, he stood around the tap awhile. Checked out the new video slots, someone showed him how they worked. Shook a few right hands. Basically no big deal. It wasn't that unusual here to run into someone after they'd been gone a long time. The fan hummed. Hooks surveyed the old walls. In summer they were crawling with flies.

Back at the nuthouse, in his dreams, he had only been able to see his friends from the waist up, talking shit and hoisting pints. He blinked as the memory swam before his eyes.

Someone smiled at Hooks from the doorway. It was Bugs. Dora and Dumb Babe were there too. Not Much settled onto his lap. It's different now, right? she said. The nuthouse?

It was different. And everyone knew it. They were pretty happy sitting there, the members of their little gang, ever changing over the years. One went away, another died, a third disappeared. But there was always someone sitting here, telling stories, somehow you were one of them. The thirtysomethings who'd survived.

Not Much knew the system as well as anyone else. All her lovers and husbands had passed through it. To stay out of the army, stay out of work, playing hide-and-seek with the cops. In the old days the nuthouse was part of the local lore. Now Hooks felt like a mastodon. But there was no need to go too deep into it.

Look, don't fuck with me, I'm tellin you straight up . . . one of the guys at the tap started in on him. Hooks, startled, sized him up. He was one of the newcomers.

Take it easy, kid . . . he said, but then caught himself and stepped on the brakes.

The new lads, who'd begun to force their way in, occasionally needed an outlet for their excess energy. Fights were different now too. There were knives. The bad boys carried guns, or gas pistols, at least. The neighborhood youth trained in stick-fighting. The tough guys strutted around draped in handcuffs and nunchucks. Fans of the band Chinese Laundry tried to take over the place at one point, probably for the drugs. They were from the quayside, though. Their guys walked around all wrapped in chains, hair dyed yellow; the girls were shaved bald. They were snobs and only smoked the green hash from Pakistan. The working-class local kids thrashed them on sight. They didn't last long.

Teenagers were no longer satisfied with cards, dice, the finally free press, and beer. A man painted pink had taken to jogging in the park. The saffron-colored saris of Buddhists swished through the dark vegetation. They came hunting souls. The stoners laughed. One kid, no older than sixteen, claimed to be a Gulf War veteran. Said his knowledge of the martial arts was what kept him young. Started recruiting. Claimed he was Korean. It worked. He employed a combined technology: drugs and videos. The foreign words most often used here, heroin and pervitin, started to get squeezed out by expressions from kung fu productions.

Nightfall in the park, dusk, which you could see out the windows here as well as from the tables outside, took its toll on even the regulars. In most pubs you can't keep track of time. Here the sun showed it to you.

The table where Hooks liked to sit resisted the tide. Every now and then, one of them went under. Most of the time they'd pop up again, eventually, step in the door, survey the room, and pull up a seat.

There's blood on the floor, Hooks said, snapping to the alert.

It's just dog blood, said Činča. From yesterday.

My dog! said Bugs. He was an elephant, I mean, not really, he was normal, but when he stepped on your foot you felt it. He was like a pit bull, but he was normal.

Hooks observed with interest: Bugs had tears gushing from his eyes. All at once. Like coins pouring out of a slot machine.

Yeah they ran him over yesterday, said Činča, so I came in here, and after our third vodka, Bugs goes, You were my buddy, but now you're my brother! Get it?

Aw, how cute, said Not Much.

I get it, nodded Hooks.

That dog always buddied around with the bitches, ever since

he was little, Činča said with a thoughtful tone. Even peed, he shot Bugs an apologetic glance, sorry but he even peed like one. Weird, right?

But Hooks's mind was on Vera. He suddenly got startled, thinking he'd seen her. But it wasn't her.

He called the cops on me! Činča said, pointing at Brownie. Can you believe it? Me!

What, are you nuts? said Brownie. If he says don't sell there, don't sell there! It's his place. So what'd the cops say?

They don't have anything on me, so nothin. How could he do that?

Don't be stupid, said Brownie. You gotta respect. That's his turf.

An what about the Ukrainians? An the Arabs? Činča wanted an argument.

That's his business, Brownie said.

I'm just glad that blood on the floor's really there, said Hooks. Then instantly apologized.

He knew he'd be going to Lyuba's tonight. And the next day too. And again after that. But what about the bleeding sky, what was he going to do about that? Let it soak into his soul. There was too much to absorb it all, though. Eventually it'd wear him down. His vision would kill him. Lyuba. Should he tell her about it? What was the use?

the sky over Angel is red
again, right now
shredded by light
clouds coiled in on themselves
I saw the sky: it was red
the wall plaster was alive
smoke rose from the pit
the sensitive asphalt was hollow
and there were people, I saw:
the sky was red

I stood and waited:
eternity whistling in the wires
whooshing through people's bones
electricity eating
things happening
I saw
and I'm watching

He was glad there was snow outside. At least that little bit. On the hill there was snow; in the city, slush. Down around the intersection hookers and pimps swarmed, perverts, addicts, rapists, like insects on an open wound. He could go there. He could stay. He could make the rounds of the game rooms, find a drug for the night, a woman, a gun, or all of it combined. With a gun he could put an end to it all. But Lyuba. He had Lyuba. And there had to be another life out there somewhere. Sometimes he had the feeling he was an emissary of that other life. That he was just here to learn . . . but then again, he'd thought the same thing back in the boiler room, with the rats. It had been going on for too long now. Maybe he had gotten lost in enemy territory. Put on the enemy camouflage and become the enemy, ready to destroy himself. That was why he saw the blood. It was a sign. That he couldn't go on like this anymore.

You guys see that freaky thing outside? I saw it once before, on the other side of the hill, someone said.

I thought it was some weird snowman, Činča laughed. But I kicked it an that's no snow.

Whatever it is, it's stupid, said Not Much. I'm done drinkin, I need coffee. Who's buyin?

When I was in the lockup, said Činča, Pelner played this joke! They had me in with Pelner. But they couldn't pin anything on us. So how do you boys make a living? cop says. And Pelner screams: I'll confess! I can't take it anymore, I want to make a confession! So they bring in the papers. Just sit in their chairs, lookin at us. I motion to him to keep his trap shut, so they pull us apart, an Pelner goes: We're murderers. I kid you not, that's what he said. Cops didn't say shit of course. They had the mikes on! That's right, Pelner goes, we're hired killers. But seein as we got weak physiques, we just use poison! Ha-hah, Činča said.

These guys are useless, said Brownie, leaning over to Hooks.

To his surprise, Hooks noticed that Brownie's face was twisted in rage.

Dumbass sells some shit to some school kids an he's just happy he's got the cash to score some for himself. It's a waste of time.

What's eatin you? asked Hooks.

I got a plan, Brownie said. But not with these guys. I need you.

What's up, boys, Not Much interrupted.

Leave us alone, said Brownie. He turned back to Hooks. I'm glad you're out. I know what you did in Paris. An get this: Vera figured it out. We figured it out.

What?

The missing element. I think we found it.

No.

Listen, said Brownie, this stuff is totally different. Unlike anything else. It changes your genetic makeup. It changes everything.

Yeah, so what? So does beer, big-time. It's all your imagination.

This stuff is bliss. An I want it. Vera wants to see you.

Yeah, me too. Some other time.

Hooks stood up, but Brownie pulled him back down to the chair.

I don't want to sell bibles, or anything else. This is the real deal. You know as well as I do we could find people with training, labs. But we wouldn't be able to keep it under wraps. This place is like Bolivia, man. Someone would take us out. We gotta start up on our own, keep it low volume. You mixed it. You were the one.

Look, all that in Paris, that's just a blur now, said Hooks. We were either high or hungover, 24-7, the whole time. Then we split up. An that's that.

That's not what Vera tells me.

I don't want that life.

You gotta mix it for us. At least once. We figured out the ingredients. We just need to test it. You're the one who mixed it. You're in danger.

What're you tryin to pull on me?

Brownie lowered his voice. Look, you guys went wild back there! There's people here, listen, believe me . . . let's just say someone's after this stuff. This shit is bliss. Someone or something with a lot of power wants it bad. Sooner or later, either way, you'll get an offer you can't refuse. You've got things you care about, right? Like anyone else! You're going to end up trapped, I'm tellin you! Like me. I'm trapped, you get it? At least now I've got money. Do it now, of your own free will, while you can. Will you do it, will you mix it? I get scared sometimes . . . believe me.

So fuck it, just walk away.

I can't, said Brownie. I know, sometimes I talk shit an stuff. But sometimes I don't know what to do. I can't walk away anymore.

Hey you . . . little nut, said Not Much. She planted herself back on Hooks's lap. What're you all huffy about? Got worries? Got woes? Just go with the flow. You must be happy, though, right? With the baby coming? Are you proud? What're you gonna call it?

Huh?

What do you mean, huh . . . you an Lyuba're havin a baby, right? I mean Lyuba's pregnant. Isn't she?

He went for a walk in the park. Wandering through the cold drizzle, kicking the snow, wet leaves. The machinery in his head was at work, spewing out stupid fantasies. Humiliating ones. All sorts of torture, tossing and turning in the fiery embers.

How come she hadn't told him? And how long had he been gone anyway?

Suddenly he froze. In between two gusts of wind, in a patch of light fallen to earth from a distant star, giving off a cold glint, he saw a face. He sharpened his gaze, then set out toward it. He got over his shock, but it wasn't a pretty sight. The statue looked like it was made of dirty white cloth, covered in splatters. Destroyed by the rain. The colors had all run into each other, with purple reigning supreme.

He noticed some pieces of paper stuck on the branches of the bushes around the statue. It reminded him of navigation races at summer camp. Orienteering. There were dozens of pieces of papers stabbed onto the branches. All over the place. He reached out to grab the nearest one, it was like the statue was watching him. The paper had printing on it. Thou shalt not steal, he read, and then: Thou shalt not commit adultery. Part of the paper was missing, probably torn by the wind. The rest of the writing was illegible, blotched by water. He snagged another, Thou shalt not kill, it said.

He let the wet papers fall to the ground. Left the others where they were. Didn't give the statue another look. Hid his freezing hands in his coat. He didn't want to linger. In the rain. He knew it was late. He rang the bell, Lyuba didn't answer. Took him awhile before he found the keys. He switched on the lights.

She staggered out of the kitchen, pants around her knees. There was blood. Coming out of her. She must've fallen. Probably fell by the window. That was where most of the blood was. She stood, swaying. He couldn't move. The blood kept coming out of her, it was on her hands, in her hair. Maybe he let out a scream. She smiled at him, lips curling back in her pale face. Right on time, she said. I was really hoping. You would be here. Right now. You almost missed it. I had a miscarriage, I think. Maybe. Quick . . . call somewhere, something.

12. The Sign

THE PARK SEEMED like a pretty good spot, Lurya thought. Not too many people, but it wasn't deserted either. He didn't want to leave the Sign where no one would see it. There was no use putting it out for no one but little boys with slingshots and rocks in their pockets. But he didn't want to leave it too much out in the open either, or the superintendents, park keepers, and cops would soon take care of it.

He brought the truck to a stop, banged on the canvas to alert his passenger, and pried himself out of the cabin with a groan. Yerya was already waiting outside, as always more eager and agile than him: Should we leave the Lord here? Is this a good spot? You don't think you chose too hastily? She greeted her companion with the same questions every time.

Lurya was ashamed to admit it to himself, but the woman rubbed him the wrong way. She was completely the opposite of the quiet, kind old lady, the first of the Faithful Lurya had met. He had sinned greatly before he became one of them. Against others and himself. Now he cultivated understanding within him. That's what they called it: cultivating understanding.

Still, sometimes Yerya's griping and moaning got on his nerves so much that he almost got carried away and forgot she was one of the Intimates. Every time they collected contributions he was reminded of it. He accompanied her, and whenever the brothers and sisters were delinquent in paying their tithes, whether due to carelessness or because they were in distress, she would rain down fire and brimstone on them with such eloquence it made his hair stand on end.

No, ma'am, this is a good spot. And we mustn't allow the Lord to flake.

Maybe that sounds disrespectful, he thought. But he couldn't help it, plaster is plaster, and the last few statues hadn't had time to harden properly yet. If they weren't careful, they might knock into each other under the canvas in back and break, the fewer there were the better. Yerya picked up one of the Signs, Lurya caught hold of the base, and together they carried it into the park.

The Sign was a statue of Christ, about five feet tall, with bulging eyes and a mouth contorted in agony. He was sculpted only from the waist up. All the Faithful cared about were his pierced heart, his murdered brain. The Christ's divine chest was graced with a lance wound, designed to issue forth an endless stream of blood, an effect achieved by means of an incision and pints of supposedly permanent red paint. But the paint was peeling off and flaking around the edges. As they dragged the statue through the bushes and along the paths, they left behind a crimson trail. Their hands were red too. The torso rested on a pedestal, hand-inscribed by initiates with the mystery of the coming.

To Lurya they were incomprehensible scratchings, but he kept that to himself. At the gatherings where the statues were inscribed with the new language, he wept and wailed along with the rest of them.

I never cease to thank the angels of the spheres that help us carry the statue, Yerya murmured, that too is a miracle. We could never do it alone.

As far as Lurya was concerned, the woman was just getting in the way, but he nodded fervidly.

Place the Sign here, Brother, Yerya said.

In the community of the Faithful to the Living Coming, all of the women were named Yerya. Lurya was the men's name. Apart from that, the Lord made no distinctions in his flock. For now, they were still living in darkness, the world was in Satan's power. Only occasionally were they able, by means of some modest gesture, to remind other people, the animal eaters, base and perverted creatures who married for money and orgasms, that the time was drawing near.

Lurya suspected his partner was higher up than him in the hierarchy of the Faithful, perhaps even very high. He knew she had left her husband and child and cast off her name. He knew she had cast off her life as a wife, as keeper of hearth and home, and filled herself with holiness to the brim. He suspected she understood the inscriptions in the new language. He was well aware of her zeal in the struggle against the impure who live with pigs and dogs. She wasn't there to lug statues around, but to speak the incantation and perform the ceremony. She was there to give orders.

Lurya hadn't come into the church thanks to clairvoyant night visions or a sudden tug of fate, but by way of a simple detour in search of hot soup and a little spare change.

It had been after the amnesty. It had been freezing. They had let thousands out of the prisons, but only some had a place to go.

The ones who had no home or took a roundabout route to get there, banded together and lived at the train stations. They lived in demolition sites on the outskirts of town, in the gutters. Some of them welcomed their unexpected freedom with thoughts of revenge. Before anything else, they wanted to settle their debts from the slammer.

Lurya shared the cell where he sliced off his ears with another man for two years. Every day, hour, second. They knew each other's every gesture, every movement, every as yet unspoken word. A man tried to kill him the very first day. But he failed. They buried him in the snow.

A few frightened citizens, especially in the smaller towns, waged pogroms against them. The outcasts gave it right back, any way they could: fire, stones, ambushes. They even attacked the police. A lot of them went back to prison.

The ones who survived the winter together allied themselves with other gangs. Sometimes they would brawl. Occasionally one of them would fail to return from his wanderings.

The old lady had come to Lurya's gang alone. She lived with them in the ruins of an old factory outside of town. Brought her own mattress. Found some cardboard boxes and built a hutch for herself among the rusted pipes. Some of the men followed her example and did the same. She cooked and mended their lice-infested rags. She put up with all sorts of crap. One day one of them shoved her into the fire, singing her hair. I'm gonna get juiced an fuck your brains out, Benio told her. She's gonna like it too, that's why she's been hittin on me, the cunt, put a hair in my soup, she's castin spells, go croak, you old bag, the Gypsy shrieked.

But as long as the quiet, modest old lady lived there with them, the police dogs and snoops seemed to stay away. The other crews made a habit of avoiding their territory. Even the weather was better all of a sudden. They always had plenty to eat. Managed to steal some clothes even. The old lady treated a wound for Benio. Pulled out a splinter of glass, just like that, nothing but her bare hands. She could set a broken bone. Even knew how to treat frostbite. With her around, it looked like they would make it through the winter without any disasters.

But then one night the superstitious Gypsy confided in Lurya that he was going to slit her throat. So Lurya, who at that time still had a different name, sent her away.

She took him with her. It was she who brought him to the Faithful, where he got his new name. Finally he could forget his prison number.

All those poor souls were set free so that you could get on the right path. You'll never live like a dog again. Said the man who baptized him.

Lurya struggled the base to the ground, staring straight into Christ's grimacing mouth.

Lurya, who had gone through life untouched by any

education, religious or otherwise, actually liked the statues. They kind of reminded him of the pictures they sold at country fairs. But the person in charge of the shop where they had cast the statues was quite likely a sadist. Or a drunk. Someone who didn't know how to deal with such an unusual order.

Jesus's ears were enormous compared to his face, flapping like sails at the sides of his head. The wound on his chest practically screamed red. His cheeks, on the other hand, were unnaturally pale, even for a dying man. It looked like he was wearing makeup. The thorns grew straight out of his forehead, jutting out like some kind of bizarre decorations. This Christ had the neck of a wrestler, with long hair like a filthy veil.

The Faithful placed the statues among the bushes in city parks, by the side of highways and small district roads. They put the Sign on the outskirts, in places where the city retreated in the face of the weeds' tenacious onslaught, which the heaps of ash, plastic, and metal sought in vain to stifle. They placed the plaster statues amid the toolsheds and fences of garden colonies, and in children's playgrounds. Not only did they guard the mighty citadel of their faith. They were also capable of attack.

When the Supreme Leaders of the Faithful denounced the election of Pope Vlk as a ruse, they took the Vatican puppets, the idols, out of the churches, and burned them in a bonfire. Lurya had carried out his assignment perfectly, slipping past the shrieking, quarreling idol worshipers with the figurine under his coat. The last thing he saw in front of the church was a woman beating her child. For stealing. Lurya smirked scornfully. Across the street from the church was a money-changing office.

The Signs were placed in view of pedestrians at unusual spots, intentionally. The Faithful believed in the power of the fleeting glance. They believed that those meant to be affected would be. They were disgusted by the Vatican puppets, worm-eaten with the sins of the old church. The same way they were disgusted by the gigantic billboards plastered with senseless objects and harlots' flesh.

For the Faithful, the statues portended that the coming of Living Salvation was near. They were magical, a center of gravity in a world buffeted by cruelty.

May the Lord come at long last and kick out Satan's eyes, Yerya moaned. Go away, Brother, leave the ceremony to me.

Lurya plodded back to the truck. They had dropped off at least ten Signs today. Only a couple left, thank God, fuckin A, Lurya grumbled to himself.

Uh-oh, he thought. But he was safe, the Sister hadn't heard. She kneeled on the ground in front of the statue, spouting the words. Squatting back on her haunches, she rolled up her skirt, then with a stained hand anointed her forehead. She touched the statue, then wiped her hand on the grass. Beat her forehead against the ground. Lurya knew she would go on like that until she was completely exhausted. Yet she never had even the slightest scrape.

Then Yerya tore up the book, spearing pieces of paper with individual words onto the branches of the sparse bushes, tossing them to the wind, some she buried in the dirt. She tore up the book, leaving it there as a message to chance passersby, cats on the prowl, the powers. What has been joined together must be put asunder. That the world may be shocked anew.

The Faithful of the Living Coming knew very well that the executioners, rapists, pornographers, drug dealers, and politicians were out to kill faith, to hound it into extinction, to ensnare human beings in the toils of fear and indifference. The Faithful knew the forces of Evil were great. But they believed that by erecting a Sign, by leaving a message here and there in the dark, they could at least offer hope.

The woman lifted her head to the sky. Despite having beat her head against the Sign and the cold-hardened ground, despite having stained herself with the greatest humiliation, which the ceremony required of the Chosen, her face was unsoiled.

Another miracle, Lurya thought.

Yerya lifted some thin black sticks out of a plastic bag. It also contained individually wrapped pieces of meat and clumps of hair. These represented the sinners who spat on the Signs. Their adversaries, who sinned against the Faithful. Lurya had a hunch what she was going to do and suspected it was going to take a while. He wasn't sure exactly what it was, but still, it made his skin crawl. He turned away. This was none of his business. He was only there to keep the ceremony from being profaned by some chance passerby.

It was almost dark out. It started to drizzle. A cold, steady rain. Not a soul around. Except a little girl walking down a path. Alone. Far away. She wouldn't disturb them. Lurya stood watch, covering. That was one thing he knew how to do.

13. We Need You

HE HAD NO idea if he wanted to be with her. No, he didn't know if he could be with her. So he accepted Machata's job offer gladly. Now he stood on a ladder, hacking into a wall. It wasn't much fun. But at least he had no problem falling asleep at night. Sometimes he'd sleep right through till morning. Pills scared him now. In fact everything scared him. He'd jump up in the air at the most ordinary sound. Maybe that was why he was enjoying making a racket now. He banged away at the joists, hacking at them till the old masonry flew. It suited him that this room in the cellar was separated from the building by a hallway. Nobody lived over there.

The flats from the old days had been partitioned off into smaller rooms, and the windows were all filled in with boards. Hooks also liked the heavy iron-plated door. It was a satisfying feeling closing it behind him, it took strength. He wondered if he could bang loud enough. If he tossed the key up the air shaft for someone to come let him out. He liked the little windows too, like arrow slits, but leading nowhere, he could watch the wall through them. Every so often he opened the door that gave onto the deserted hallway and aired the room out. During the war it had been a shelter. A lightbulb hung from the ceiling. Sometimes Hooks huddled up in there like a rabbit. Sometimes he paced, wall to wall, like a Siberian tiger. Often he alternated back and forth between the two.

He climbed down from the ladder. Time to wash up and get out. To see Lyuba, like he did now every day.

A child. Hadn't counted on that, he'd never seen any kids in his dreams. It also kind of upset him that he couldn't be sure it was his. The new being Lyuba so desperately clung to inside her. They'd both gotten used to it, it was part of their lives. But Hooks didn't know. The only thing he knew for sure was he couldn't live in her flat just yet. Also, there was no phone here.

He had dragged a mattress into the room and taken up residence. Machata was elated to get his hands on such cheap labor.

A storeroom's what I need most, young fella. Of course you can stay here, for now. Seein as your bride-to-be is the owner an all. Your soon-to-be missus, heh heh heh. Nothin gets past me! the shopkeeper smiled.

The missus meanwhile was tied down. Hooks, in his hospital shoe covers, stole up on her silently, like a desert animal. He was a master when it came to that, having learned his way around the linoleum of hospitals, nuthouses, and jail cells at a tender age. In rare moments, out of view of the authorities, he even got in a tap dance or two in the corner. But he knew it wouldn't be right to tap-dance in the hospital he was visiting now, since the ruling local authority here, death, was a constant presence.

Sliding as quickly as possible through the dimly lit corridors of the maternity ward, he avoided the women in various stages of carving and abandonment. With the Christmas holidays approaching, the only ones left in the hospital were those who really had to be. Or those with nowhere to go.

welcome to hell
ladies first
like always like usual
like up there
like in civil society
among the demons

The worst part, Lyuba told him, was when they strapped me to the horse, legs in the air. Then I put em back down an one of the doctors, the nice one, goes: Pardon me, ma'am, but your foot is in the bucket. I had my foot, this one right here, she pointed . . . in the bucket.

What bucket?

The one where they throw the embryos an stuff. The placenta, all that stuff from inside. I couldn't stop crying.

Uh-huh. Sorry to hear. So is the kid mine, or not?

I think so. You've just gotta take it for what it is.

Uh-huh.

Lyuba was obviously feeling better. She'd lost that chalky paleness that made her nose stick out so strangely from her face.

Hooks had been a little drunk when he brought her in, by cab. As it turned out, the head nurse, the only one at the reception desk, had a few in her too.

They both instantly scented it on each other, and while Lyuba was incapable of saying a word or taking a step, Hooks and the head nurse communicated via the surreptitious signals of pragmatic alcoholics. The language of the perpetually at-risk. The language of animals who survive their hunters, the traps and the high-voltage wires. The language of the endangered species of urban degenerate Old World monkeys.

The head nurse's total cynicism formed a protective shield against the unspeakable horror that Lyuba might outright expire in his arms. Despite the tragic weight of the situation and the physical weight of the woman he bore in his arms, Hooks felt an instinctive attraction toward the head nurse. Together they handed the unconscious Lyuba over to a little doctor, who seemed to have been off somewhere hiding from cases like hers. All Hooks saw after that was the back of some stooped paramedic as he carted Lyuba off to the operating room.

He attempted to stop him, but the head nurse scolded Hooks, assured him everything would be fine, gave him a wink, and said to get lost. Please call back tomorrow and now stop being a nuisance.

He walked home through the night, the whole way

convinced that the most unspeakable acts of indecency were going on behind locked doors in every building, rampant obscenity, perhaps even murder. The mist and darkness amid the flash of traffic lights, the occasional flicker across the cobblestones from the cracks in windows and doorways, were a shem in the Golem's mouth, their mysterious effect bringing to life fantastical beings. The moon, high above, stewed in the vapors. Psychosis made a tenacious play for the potential future father. He even heard stealthy footsteps behind him, furtive shuffling. Maybe someone was trying to kill him, he thought, bash his head in with a cobblestone. It could be.

Around four in the morning he stopped in one of the game rooms by the intersection. It was lively. He blinked. After what he'd seen in the hospital. He stood there, looking calm. After what had happened to Lyuba. It was Saturday and this was the life after life. Random citizens, local hoodlums, all variety of strays, drinking themselves silly. It was Saturday, end of the week, no more fighting, no more dealings, Saturday morning and Friday night, just one big hole. Intermission. Till the whole thing starts back up again. Arriving by tram.

Some of the clientele were just dozing, others were anesthetizing restless scars, bandaging over scratches, wounds. Only to open them up again the next day, and take a look around for the nearest saltshaker too. A whole advanced industry existed solely for that purpose.

Hooks looked around him. The flagging party was getting back up to speed. There were people he knew here too. He could have confided in Dora, Steffi. It probably would've been a relief to talk with a woman right now. But they were busy.

Even with their amazing win on Telebingo, the two little sisters had kept their jobs as waitresses. Now they were enjoying themselves.

Činča stood, in a drunken stupor, back leaned up against the target. They also had him propped up with a chair. Dumb Babe was outlining his body with darts. The whizz of the dart and the light thunk as it sunk into the target. And again! Right next to his ear. Steffi and Dora took turns throwing too. The dudes at the bar, draped in gold chains, applauded. Hooks looked on, intrigued. He even considered taking a throw himself. The way Činča's tongue was hanging out of his mouth, with one well-aimed shot he could pin it right to the target. The idiot wasn't even making any noise. Strange game, humiliating a man to the nth degree. And they were just getting warmed up.

One drunken dude sank a dart into Činča's belly, another stuck him in the shoulder. His leather jacket took the brunt. Dora and Steffi came out from behind the bar, Dumb Babe did a little dance around Činča. Tie him up, someone suggested. Another dart stabbed him through his pants, he began to come around. Steffi, pulling darts out of the target around Činča's woozy head, couldn't contain herself, grabbed him by the hair and planted a kiss on his lips. That evoked a storm of laughter.

Amid the ensuing euphoria, throwers lined up along the bar and showered him in a rain of darts. Hooks felt queasy, he had no interest in seeing blood. A scuffle broke out in the corner. Let the girls throw! shouted the bouncer. The girls stepped up to the bar, darts clenched in their fists. Some troublemaker tried to take advantage of the fact that they were preoccupied to make a grab for the bottles. The regulars stepped in to prevent the theft. A muffled cry, a few quick moves, and next thing you know, the floor was covered in broken glass. Darts whizzed in every direction. Dora had an honest-to-goodness nervous breakdown. Uh! said Činča.

In short: If by divine dispensation some random medievalist, on his drive back to the airport, still dazed by the lengthy applause bestowed upon him by attendees of the international congress for his fittingly titled "Remarks on the Origin, Evolution, and Pauperization of Ghettos in Central and Eastern Europe," had succumbed to the urge to stop in for a quick drink, he might well have believed that he had walked right into the raging midst of an orgy of a previously unknown sect of Sebastianites.

Just then the drunken saint finally let out a yell, he'd been hit. Hooks took advantage of the confusion to duck out without paying. A little less than an hour later he groped for his jangling phone. It was Vera. He slammed down the receiver. The second time he picked up.

Well, how's she doing? Your little sweetiekins? Huh?

He had definitely heard right. It was his partner from the underground passages of Nurreille.

What? he said. How do you know?

I have my ways. Let's just say a friend of yours saw the two of you together.

What do you want?

You know what I want.

I'm not in the mood.

Don't worry, she'll pull out of it. You have no idea what women can take. When they want to. When they've got a reason.

I feel sick.

Aw, poor boy. We figured out there's only three things it could be, three substances. The missing component!

Not me, not interested.

Hooks heard some kind of scuffle on the other end. He lit up a smoke. The dim light of early morning filled the room.

Hey there! Brownie's voice boomed into the phone. It pissed Hooks off for some reason. That he was there. That he was with Vera.

You don't mind if we stop by, right? You need your friends at a hard time like this! And we . . . we need you.

Hooks felt like he was suffocating. That was the worst possible thing he could imagine. He didn't want to see them. He didn't want to see anybody.

Leave me alone.

Just five minutes, pleaded Brownie. We got it narrowed down to three things . . .

Hooks slammed down the phone. He'd barely recovered

when he pictured Lyuba again. Her blood-drained face. Her finely shaped nose sticking out like a hideous beak. Like some old ladies have. Never before had she felt so heavy in his arms. He took a rag and wiped up the blood in the kitchen. Then moved on to the entranceway. The doorbell rang. He'd made up his mind, if it was Brownie he'd throw him out.

He pulled back the blind to check. The sun was coming up, the dawn's red skies blinded him, falling cruelly into his eyes, a horde of miniature red devils. The wall of sunlight came from the opposite side, over the hill, broken up into shiny flashes. Red skies like a storm of red darts, dots, small animals, a dawn of insects. He blinked, rode it out. The bell rang again. He washed off his hands, then opened the door for the patiently waiting Machata.

14. Where Does It Hurt?

Saw you had your lights on, neighbor, said Machata, snow scraper in hand. He shook off the metal tool, knocked the damp lumps of snow from his shoes. It's better to get up early, squeeze more work in that way, you know, nowadays . . . he said, crowding into the entranceway. Sorry bout what happened to the young missus, hope you don't mind I call her missus, yeah they're all little shits these days anyway. Least my girl's healthy. Ever since my missus left, Machata rattled on mercilessly to the uncomprehending Hooks, missus Lyuba's done a great job of lookin after my Nadia, yep. They're practically best friends! Nadia, the little chickie, she's not mine either. Healthy, well, apart from the fact that she never talks an never grows, not an inch taller than the day we got her. Always hangin around, never goes anywhere, that's our Nadia, you know how she is. Am I right or aren't I?

Hooks had known Machata ever since he'd first opened his shop and never could stand him. He knew he gave his girl a sound beating, regularly.

What can I do for you? he said. He wasn't about to invite the guy in.

Well the thing is, missus Lyuba an me, we had sort of a deal between us, Machata said, opening up, it was obvious he felt more at home in the masculine realm of business than in the sensitive minefield of subtle condolences. An I was wondering if maybe, uh, wouldn't mind one of those myself! Machata said as Hooks opened the fridge and took out a bottle of beer. He handed one to Machata too. The shopkeeper sat down in a chair and lit up a smoke. Hooks pondered how to get rid of him. But his neighbor was just getting started.

I'm expandin my business, y'know. Put up some promotions to start: "Eats you can't beat, powders too, clothes galore, smokes for you. Sundries, Richard Machata wholesaler, Prague 5 – Košíře." What do you think, huh? Got that kid from the pub here to paint the sign! You know the one. I want something people can relate to, none of that "sekendhend USA sendvič" crap. I sell Czech-made products for Czechs, damn it! It's long, I know, an the powders thing sounds funny. But I want a drugstore too, you know? Machata tapped his ashes on the floor. An dishwashing powders, that's a mouthful. Machata snuck a peek at his silent host. The ice still wasn't broken.

Oh I get it, you're what do they call it, in shock, aren't you, neighbor? Hm, yeh-yeh. Then there's my old lady, I think she went right off the deep end, we men got it tough. Yeah, she left me. Nadia too. What do you say we go for a drink sometime, or twenty, right? Thing is, there's this one other flat still, slightly demolished. Not here on this street, down there, other side of Angel Station. Past the intersection. Missus Lyuba owns that building too, yeh. That down there's Smíchov, but I mean Smíchov, Košíře, same thing, right? One big happy family! So I expand to Smíchov! Hop skip an a jump. An missus Lyuba said I could, like, convert it into a storeroom. That's the thing. An so what I wanted to ask you was whether, I mean, y'know . . . I need to expand my shop. Little Nadia an me can barely take a step in our place as is, what with all the junk . . . thing is, if missus Lyuba, like, what do you call it . . . if you get my drift . . .

If she dies, would I rent it to you? said Hooks.

Yeah.

Get the hell out! Fuck off!

Now hold on there . . . hooold on, Machata the bear agilely slipped out of his chair. There was a gleam in his eyes. He surged toward the door, keeping Hooks, mid-stride, safely at bay. Arms at his side, didn't even lift a finger. Hooks checked his rage. For all Machata's clumsiness, it dawned on Hooks, underneath he still had the quick, economical movements of a seasoned pub brawler.

Sorry, said Hooks. He collapsed back into his chair.

Nah . . . no need, listen, now that we've gotten to know each other, I'm sorry too, young fella, stoppin by like this so soon. Y'know, that little girl of mine cries for missus Lyuba! The competition might come visit, an missus Lyuba an me, we had a deal. An folks've been askin about her. You'd be surprised! Stop by sometime. Lots of young folks from the neighborhood hang around my shop. Friends of yours! They want to talk with you. An from what I hear, you don't want to talk with them. You'd be surprised how highly they think of missus Lyuba! Ask about her all the time. An you too! I know, you were gone a long time. Well, come on by. Or I'll come by. I mean we're neighbors, right? We'll work something out, I can tell, I got a nose for these things. Wouldn't've come this far without it.

It turned out he was right. Hooks didn't go see him in the shop. But they did reach an agreement.

His work in the future storeroom helped keep him afloat. The whole thing sank in slowly, swirling around his head. He moved in his couple bags of clothes and a hotplate. It was hard for him being in Lyuba's flat without her. Being with her might be even harder, he realized. Nor did he have the slightest interest in meeting with Brownie and Vera. She wouldn't stop calling.

We need you, she'd say insistently. And Brownie got angrier and angrier every time.

Just do it, she said. I'm tellin you cause I still love you. You don't know how bad they want this stuff. Something's gonna happen. I know it. Please. Don't be so stubborn.

The sadness in her voice surprised him. But he slammed down the phone. He had no intention of doing it. He wasn't about to mix bliss again. Instead he made a move. Into the storeroom.

He hacked away at the partitions in the flat. Sometimes Machata worked with him. Nadia, though . . . something about that girl terrified Hooks. She would watch them sometimes while they worked. Just stand and stare. Since she'd lost her dog it seemed like she had gotten even smaller. As if she herself were turning into a little animal. She didn't respond even when Hooks cracked the occasional joke. To tell the truth, he could have used a few laughs himself. He had a feeling the only time the girl really listened to him was when he talked about Lyuba. She always said to tell the girl hello. He never mentioned his wife in front of the shopkeeper.

Nadia stood around the empty hallway, playing with the metal-plated doors, running up and down the street, poking around the house. Hooks had long since given up on trying to figure out what was going through her head. Her presence made him nervous. But when he went a long time without seeing her, he would get uneasy. It was enough just to know she was around.

And afternoons he was back in his shoe covers, sliding along the linoleum.

So guess what, there's a new orderly, an he says if I'm here over the holidays, I'll get a room to myself.

That's great. Where does it hurt?

Everywhere.

Christ, don't they give you shots?

All the time.

Hm.

So you know what's weird about it?

What?

You don't get used to the pain. I mean when it's a little, yeah, but not when it's a lot. I hear you're livin in Machata's storeroom. What's up with that?

Not livin . . . just spendin time. Thinkin an stuff.

You're just waiting for me to get well enough so you can take off again. That's truly admirable of you.

No, it's not that. Cross my heart.

What about your little Vera?

I haven't seen her.

Bullshit. You call each other?

No.

More bull. How bout that little girl, Nadia, poor thing.

She's an odd one. Should I bring her by? So are you still pregnant or not?

They say I still am. This one time I got the feeling they weren't sure. But that's impossible, right? They've been taking blood. Lots of it. The head nurse is talking about a caesarean. Cutting me open. If it survives. Better not bring the girl, might freak her out. What about Vera, though? So she can see. We could all meet here. Then again that might freak you out.

They gonna cut you open?

I don't know. Don't ask me. I can take it.

Anything I should bring?

No.

They worked in the storeroom every day now. Women can take a lot, said Machata, laying out the augers, gimlets, handsaws, tools of the trade. Some of them Hooks didn't even know existed.

Don't worry bout that woman of yours. Missus Lyuba, she can take it. My first wife, she dumped me too, go figure. Over a guy, not for nothing. I was out of my mind. So I found myself a cute girl from Libeň. Later my first one came back. Whorin around. Where else would she go? She had no place. So I said OK, but piss me off an you're gone. Yep, that was a long time ago, pass the spatula! Then my girl from Libeň took me to a fortune-teller, that was illegal in those days, I forked over two hundred crowns. An she predicted my old lady would come back. Not out of love, mind you, but livin with me she was safe. Course I believed it, so soon as my first wife started pissin me off, I tossed her out. Turns out that girl from Libeň had paid the card reader five hundred crowns to tell me that. Stupid me. Quick, pass me that tin snip!

Right.

Do you believe in fortune-tellers?

Never met one.

That one I saw, she's dead now. I don't believe in it either. Made this glue myself, for stucco. Yeah an my last one walked out, she latched onto faith. Now all I got's Nadia, my little princess. Not much of a talker. But she'll be good in the store. She can sell anything. That girl knows what she's doin, all right . . . an won't say a word to anyone. Check out that glue, huh? Made it myself. See how it holds?

Yep. Amazing.

What'd I tell you.

During the day he worked on the storeroom, sometimes with Machata, sometimes alone, moped around the neighborhood, kicked around the intersection. Glanced up at the red sky, into it. Saw the clouds, the light that blazed through them. Saw other lights too. Roamed around the pit.

One evening he was on his way back to his new lair, the storeroom, his shelter, walking down the street, sticking close to the walls and dodging the puddles, he knew that come spring, beneath the dirty snow and black lumps of ice, the limp mockwort would sprout in some spots and the vallonias would come crawling out, nature from the earth's insides . . . and there on the corner stood Vera.

Her hair had grown back in. It was even starting to curl gently along the sides.

The next thing he knew, they were sitting across from each other again.

So my patience paid off, she said, stirring the spoon in her coffee.

I'm glad to see you too. It'd be amazing if you guys'd just stop hassling me about that stuff.

Hm, Vera smiled.

Hooks had the thought that he deeply hated her. Then he dipped within himself again and, with a peculiar blend of fear and amazement, discovered he wanted to kiss her. And did.

Hmmm, she stretched afterward. And here I was thinkin I was going to hate you till the day I died. For leavin me there like that. I was a total wreck. Totally ragged out, wiped. If it hadn't been for Vladimir, I probably would've ended up sellin my ass on the streets or something.

So you didn't?

You pig. Nut.

Not really. Just tryin to save myself.

Me too, friend. Me too. An it'd be nice if our efforts didn't get in each other's way. Don't you think?

Then they went to the storeroom. Over the following days, they both started to have the same dream: They were crossing legs with each other, high up in the air. It was mysterious and nice. They were scared.

But mostly he just wandered around the neighborhood on his own. Brownie stopped calling and Vera kept quiet. But it was there between them. He knew she wanted it. Three substances, he asked her one night. What are they, which ingredients? Why does it have to be me?

Will you mix it?

No. Why me?

How's Lyuba? She asked him that often now. You been to see her?

What're the substances?

Will you do it?

No.

Then give it a rest. All in good time. Go see Lyuba. You need her. She needs you.

15. The Dark

A NEW GAME room opened up on the street, two blocks from where he and Machata were building the storeroom. There were hookers standing out in front. The go-getter who owned the place threw up a sign in the passageway, slapped some plaster onto the dying wall, and hung out his shingle: cafe. You could barely see it.

This one stands in place, that one strolls the sidewalk, she's got red leggings. The fat one there stomps her feet to keep from freezing, in summer she'll sit on a stool, nod to you. And keep that one in your dreams, boy. And go on home, she's out of your league. Cars, vendors. Coins in the gutter, coins seen through the sewer grate. When it rains, even the few insects that somehow make it through the winter thaws disappear. Crawl out of sight, go into hiding.

That one's got a blond braid, sits around the café with her baby sometimes. That skinny one there's Romanian or Slovenian, she's new. At first she stood with the others, twittering amid the flock, bumming change, a cigarette, now she stands on the corner alone, head hung, kicking the curb with her sneaker.

What'll it be? Bugs hollers to Hooks. Goin out tonight? Cold, huh?

Nasty. I'm not goin anywhere. Gimme some tokens.

Hooks is playing that awesome game, seriously it's the best one ever.

Terminator leads the robot ranks against his warriors, Hooks blows them to bits, a couple fighters of his take a hit. There are six, hiding out in the ruins of the city. He scores seven thou. Not bad. Bugs is the only one who can get over ten. He tells

Hooks stories about the kids who come in to play. Hooks has seen them around, they hit him up for change, sometimes when he plays the game they line up behind him. He keeps tabs on the light pressure in the place where his wallet should be.

That's Guinea Pig, Bugs points out a scrawny ten-year-old in a nylon running top. Kid's got a tic, bares his teeth, actually looks like a guinea pig.

Scored twenty thou, says Bugs. An that little Gypsy kid, that's Baby Jesus. That's his apprentice, Bugs laughs.

Bullshit! No way. I still can't break eight.

Yeah but that's all he does all day, Bugs laughs. Wanna know how it ends?

How?

When you hit twenty thou, the Hairy Guy commits suicide.

Hairy Guy is the best out of the six warriors. He's got the most powerful energy sources.

Give him a Coke on me, Hooks gestures to Guinea Pig. Give em both a Coke, he decides generously, tossing a coin on the table.

The blonde stood and went upstairs, baby in her arms. It started crying.

Lyuba's bad off. Sometimes she doesn't even talk. Ever since they took her child away from her, dead. He's finally getting used to how pale her face is. But today it's her voice that bothers him. Like it isn't even hers.

They're really nice to me here, she told Hooks. That new orderly promised he'd put in a TV for me. An that old lady, the one that washes the floors, you know what she said? She said little kids who die like that go straight to heaven. She believes in God. I always thought God was just a word, Lyuba said in her different voice. Or an interjection. Like when you're dying. But that's the kind of thing you start thinking about when you're in here. The head nurse keeps chasing her away. She does my IV too. Even takes my blood herself. But I'll pull through, don't worry. That old lady gave me this, she said it'd help, Lyuba said, showing him the object.

Heaven, huh? said Hooks. So it's in heaven? Maybe the medication was making her voice like that. She'd never talked that slow before.

That's right. Naked up there with the animals. In paradise. All the little kids. No one can hurt them up there. They're safe. It must've hurt a lot down here.

An how bout you?

She had tears coming out of her eyes. But that was the whole time he'd been there, maybe even before.

Me? Whatever, I lived. I've done bad things too. I cry all the time. I just can't get used to it.   Hooks panicked a little, tried to get hold of the doctors. Looked around for the head nurse. Then went back to Lyuba.

Go home, she told him the same thing as everybody else. You can't do anything here. You can't help.

She gripped the figurine tightly in her hand.

She said it would help, Lyuba told him. It's worth a try. Right? She looked into his eyes, then her eyes slid down, along the pillow to the wall, and stayed there.

Hooks slogged his way down the street with no energy, not even the slightest spark, numb with the specific pain of being male and powerless. He didn't even try to avoid the intersection.

Angel Exit. At the time, he thought he knew all there was to know about the red sky. But then he spotted Nadia.

He was riding past in the tram, and there, by the pit where the people disappeared, he spotted her. He was ready to call out to her, jump off the moving car, but she stopped at the edge of the pit and stood. She stood, and a moment later the crowd covered her from view.

Hooks shrugged, he knew the people eater spared a few here and there. Nadia. He had no idea why. He got off at the next stop, taking in the sounds of the trams, their clanging, the

voices of the street, the radio, all the other sound waves, and
thought of the horses. The horses that had pulled wagons here
until not long ago; when they slaughtered them, they chopped
the hooves off the carcasses and boiled them down. For glue.
He knew that.

As he passed by the synagogue, he could smell the urine.
How many generations of drunks had pissed there since the
war. Under the archway, against the battered door. There were
flyers posted there, he deciphered the letters and found out: The
Perun Society was accepting female members, the Association
for a More Beautiful and Dutiful Prague was growing, and the
Tatra Smíchov Boxing Club was promoting total calm. He
read that they were hiring grinders and millers for the rail and
tramcar factories. He weighed his chances and dismissed them.

He stepped out of the way as three little boys dragged a
floppy-eared mastiff into his path. They each had their own
leash attached to the dog. As Hooks stepped back, he nearly
slammed into a cop who had stopped a rundown character
lugging a sack of potatoes. They were tumbling out all over the
place. A little old lady in a headscarf deftly snagged a few choice
spuds. The cop snickered, waved his hand, the character moved
along.

People stared out the window of the McDonald's. Hooks
wondered if one of them might be giving him a sign. He saw a
shadow, a hand went up. He went over to investigate, stopped
a few inches shy of the pit. Just. False alarm. His heart started
pounding. He lifted his head. He knew what he would see above
the whole ever-changing amoeba-like set, the stage of everyday
life, you might say, was an inscription carved in Hebrew and
Czech: "Peace, peace to him that is far off, and to him that is
near." Oh, definitely. Definitely, Hooks thought to himself.

Hand me those square shanks, Machata hollered at him from
the scaffolding. We're gonna stretch that mesh out good.

The last thing they were putting up was the nylon insect

netting.

Yep, flesh flies they call em, little black things. All kinds of things rot in the air shaft, you know. You wouldn't believe it, just the other day in the garbage I found a . . . I don't even know what. Bang that thing in, right here. An with the kind of people we got runnin around here these days, scary, said Machata, the upright entrepreneur.

Good girl, he praised Nadia and took back the hammer. What would we do without you, hon, huh? Hooks held the net in place while Machata took the hammer and nails and pounded, with all his might, hammering it down.

Meat eaters, these flies an mosquitos! Just wait'll you see em swarmin up from the river come summer. I block off the shaft here an there's no flies gettinin this ointment, no sir!

They attached the mesh, but Hooks still had a feeling some other creature might come up the shaft, to get to the flies and mosquitoes. Something the mesh wouldn't stop, but just slice into little bits for a second and then they would join back together again. Or something that would pass right through it, like a hot breath of air.

Whenever he couldn't sleep, he would listen to the sounds of the light well, the bubbling from inside it, the tenants' radios and dueling toilets, the drunks vomiting and women weeping and teenage girls shrieking, he heard blood spatter into a bowl, a dry cough change to a death rattle.

The sounds came down the air shaft along with the sour vapors of their gas stoves and the muggy nighttime heat of their illegal space heaters. Through the shaft he could hear and smell every one of the people as they turned out the lights at night, one after the other, and the darkness made its way to him. But also, through the walls, he could sense a light rising from the people, a trace of something, some unknown substance, that all-powerful secret ingredient that makes life life, he could sense it, and the darkness all around was thick and murderous, but it hadn't swallowed the people up. Or him either.

16. Where Is Li

Li was getting nervous. He wasn't in a laughing mood. Li rarely laughed. Besides, he was at work now. And his work was killing people. But he was nervous. He didn't quite know where he was.

He didn't know what this neighborhood was called. He came from the nation that had invented the mirror, but he had no idea of the invention's effect on the locals. On the people in the buildings around him. On the territory he had been assigned to investigate.

The name of the Prague district Smíchov took hold the morning the local citizens truly saw themselves for the first time. Which came about thanks to the charity of the upstart Klestka, a spirits smuggler.

At the beginning of the century, Klestka had undertaken a pilgrimage to the Convent of Baba Sava, in the region known as Lusatia, and there was granted the grace of conversion and saw the light. He asked Baba Sava, or rather her incarnation, how he could best repent for his numerous sins, and was challenged to live a life so exemplary that even his sinful neighbors would have to look themselves in the face. That, the incarnation of Baba Sava informed him, would also be the surest way to bring about their conversion.

Thus, through the charity and generosity of the upstart Klestka, a great mirror was installed in every household in the vicinity, near and far. Until then, the only way that people could get a glimpse of themselves was by paying a kreuzer to look in a pocket mirror, or maybe a puddle, or the eternally streaked shiny surface at the one local barber. There were no mirrored locks or still clean-water surfaces for miles around. And there still aren't.

True, the gift was not an entirely charitable act on Klestka's part. He knew the mirrors would evoke envy beyond the district's borders, in the streets leading from the intersection up into the steep hills.

That neighborhood is called Košíře. At the turn of the eighteenth century it was founded by a group of Gypsy families who made their living mainly from their masterfully woven baskets and mats. For the giant baskets known as kokory, however, they needed reeds. The inhabitants of Smíchov demanded a fee from them to pass through the neighborhood to the muddy banks of the Vltava. And this created tension.

The inhabitants of Košíře were proud of their splendid, brightly colored mats, which decorated the walls of even the neediest dwellings. Even the poorest day laborer's home was graced with at least one enchanting rug. Into each mat the skillful weavers and braiders wove entire stories, believed to originate from the cradle of basket weaving and mat making in India.

These rugs and mats depicted unheard-of animals and exotic tropical flowers. Even a full day after their completion, they continued to give off a heavy, intoxicating perfume. Often the mats featured renderings of ancient gods; many portrayed women and men at the moment of merger. Wild rumors circulated in Prague about the secret rituals that accompanied their giving. But even the mats' fame was surpassed by the gift of the parvenu smuggler Klestka, who went on to be a distiller. The mirrors, which were the height of a medium-sized adult man, were a genuine sensation. And the people saw themselves.

That morning, the recipients of the gift, scrubbed, eager and dressed in their best, stood before the new mirrors, whole families gathered, and when they saw . . . legend has it that that morning the local constables were startled by a thunderous explosion of laughter—smích, in Czech. And ever since then, the city landscape around the intersection has been known as Smíchov.

It's certainly no coincidence that the name owes its existence to the alertness of the police, given that it served to designate the restless zone between the river and the intersection—a place where, sometimes, people disappear—and that it was above that intersection that Rabbi Leraya one day saw his spiritual teacher, Abraham Angel, floating; Abraham Angel, walking across the sky, high above the believers, they almost threw out their necks . . . Angel nodded to the pious flock, it was a sign . . . for at that very moment, there was a massive wave of refugees swelling, primarily Hasidic Poles fleeing the plague of Cossack marauders. And Rabbi Leraya, renowned for his wisdom and erudition far beyond the borders of his own now razed and pillaged shtetl, had been summoned to Prague by the elders of the Smíchov community.

That morning, as the learned rabbi later recounted, the laughter floated above the rooftops, gathered in strength, then seemed to suffer a cramp, suddenly going stiff in mid-air and falling to the ground in the form of hailstones . . . that memorable morning the rabbi, riding in his carriage filled with women, children, and cackling baby geese, saw the Angel and ordered his carriage to stop. He rose, stepped to the ground, touched his head to the earth in gratitude, and ordered a collection to be taken up. The money allowed the Prague city councillors to be paid off, and Rabbi Leraya was able to remain with his flock.

And in memory of the apparition the wise rabbi had a synagogue erected on the intersection, which is called Angel to this day.

Li knew none of that. And it didn't interest him either. He was a refugee from a Communist country, he'd never lived anywhere legally in his life, and everywhere they sent him he made his living doing what he had known best ever since his early youth: violence. He had a memory for faces, it was part of his profession. He used to see the man he was following now in and around the underground passages in Nurreille, where he had been responsible for guarding certain workshops. When Li was dispatched to this city, to explore the opportunities here, he encountered the man his very first day, in the early morning hours.

It struck him as suspicious. So he decided to follow him. Maybe he should have killed him. Instead he had thrown away the cobblestone in his hand. If he'd used it, his worries would have been over now. But most likely it was nothing more than a coincidence, a figment of his imagination, like a dream, and the man really did live here now.

For several days, Li followed Hooks from the storeroom to the hospital and back. He had to make sure. Li didn't care about him or his friend's business. The man was a harmless nut. And the woman was obviously dying. Li shrugged. He didn't understand what they were doing to her in the hospital. His assignment was to follow Hooks. So he also saw what they did to the woman when she was alone in her room. That was none of his business.

17. The Trap

HOOKS WALKED IN, but no Lyuba. The bed in her room was freshly made, not a wrinkle. Not a thing anywhere, just some marks on the linoleum, probably from all the IVs. He walked back out, knocked on the nurse's door, meekly, as he'd been taught. He opened the door, no one there either, just a movie playing on the TV with the sound turned off. He saw Christmas trees, people.

He stood in the corridor, no one walked by, none of the women he normally saw were sitting on the wooden bench, standing by the window with their enormous bellies . . . even the old cleaning lady, standing around all the time like she was on guard, even she was gone, it was Christmastime, a small tree stood in the corner of the corridor, someone had hung bells on it.

A couple plates of leftover food sat on a small table covered with plastic wrap, Hooks looked, wrinkled his nose, definitely old . . . then he knocked on the door of the next room down, stepped inside. Stood there alone, for the first time. No one in the office either, typewriters were covered up, polished floor shone like a spaceship . . .

Quietly, cautiously, he walked the corridors, this was a safe zone for women, wholly under the protection of the puzzling women's demon, puzzling because he not only protected, but also dealt out blows, sometimes suddenly, without warning, sometimes strangling the victim slowly as he turned the screws on the torturous rack of his chilling body. Measuring out the doses of life and pain to the pregnant in their multiplied solitude as he alone saw fit, the demon of hair and skin and insides, who made a pact with the first woman . . . and the sole visitor quietly slipping through the corridors suddenly saw him in his mind, just for a second catching sight of his flattened serpent's head, yellow eyes.

He wandered the corridors, took a peek inside the head nurse's office too. The blinds were drawn and it was totally dark. Even the lights in the corridors seemed dimmed to him.

He went back to Lyuba's room and realized all he could do now was wait. An eternity. He knew all he could do was wait, but he didn't know what for. He had known something might happen. But he hadn't really understood what it was. The hell inside him was emptiness, he coiled up in it. Waiting.

The door opened, she walked in slowly, limping, neither of them said a thing, then she was next to him, gripping his sleeve, the cleaning lady.

You're early today, good thing, the old woman said softly. And be quick. When I tell you.

Is she dead? said Hooks.

Go now! said the woman, pointing to the door. He obeyed as if in a dream.

He stood in the corridor and saw . . . kicked off his shoe covers, saw the bare feet, saw the body under the sheet and caught sight of the face, kicked off his shoe covers and broke into a run.

They pushed the gurney with Lyuba on it into the room at the end of the corridor, nothing but a lightbulb hanging from the ceiling, the morgue. They pushed the gurney with Lyuba lying on it into the morgue. Hooks yanked open the door, shoved the head nurse out of the way, and saw Lyuba's pale face. She was breathing and her eyes were open. The ambulance driver jumped back, startled, stood looking at Hooks, all hunched over, uh . . . he said.

There's nothing wrong with her, I swear, there's nothing wrong, shouted Vladimir.

He's tellin the truth, for real! said another voice, it was

Brownie, cautiously, oh so cautiously rolling the gurney a tad further into the room, so it stood between him and Hooks, on his left the head nurse, on his right Vladimir, their old pal, who had suddenly appeared out of nowhere, he lifted his hands, apparently preparing to speak . . . which he could have, since Hooks had fallen silent. Under his hand he could feel Lyuba's warm knee, he had instinctively grabbed hold of it. And he wasn't about to let go of it now.

She really must've been on medication, because Hooks couldn't believe . . . that she'd feel so at home in the hospital. That she'd wait. For the little song and dance they were giving him now, explaining to him so nicely. He knew she wasn't on their side. And he knew very well she was suffering because of him. Him and his stubbornness. That was the first thing they told him too. Shouting over one another.

And, in his own interest, later on, he never did tell the doctor about what happened in the morgue.

Christmas, you know, almost no one's around, Brownie leered at him in the cab. Lookin forward to Santa?

You know, I really did help her out, man, said Vladimir, she had her own private room with a TV!

There was just no other way to get through to you, said Brownie. You wouldn't listen an there was no other way to make you see how bad we want this thing.

Yeah, this was the only way, Vladimir chimed in . . . to make it clear.

It took us a while to figure out the third ingredient, Brownie went on. We tried everything, believe me! But now it's obvious.

The only thing obvious to Hooks now was that they wanted the drug so badly they would've killed Lyuba, easy. And him too, no sweat. And why not him? What did they need him so bad for?

For Chrissake, Brownie, I can't believe you'd actually kill for this stuff.

Are you crazy, c'mon, it was just a joke . . .

No, you'd never pull a joke that sick on me. An the kid, you rat . . . how could you do that to Lyuba?

You made us! You know I'd never kill anyone.

Oh no? Alright then, driver, I'm getting out . . .

Brownie grabbed him by the wrist and whispered: Yeah, I'd do anything, I don't give a fuck. Either give it to us or I kill Lyuba. An if I don't do it, Vladimir or the head nurse will. Or somebody else. You don't stand a chance. Go ahead an call me a monster. But you have no idea. This is paradise. Paradise for everyone on earth. Sheer bliss. Seriously.

So what do you need me for?

You'll find out.

Cause I'm the first one who mixed it?

You an Vera.

18. The Storeroom

VERA WAS WAITING for him. In the storeroom. Standing there, under the lightbulb, arms crossed on her chest, smiling. There was a gas stove. The old familiar flasks, beakers, and vials. The kind of setup you might call Little Chemist or Big Junkie, depending. All of Hooks's old glassware was there. Plus a few modern improvements. All sorts of contraptions. Vera always did have a head on her. Clever girl, reliable: Reformatory Queen, Virgin Mistress, Butcherette Extraordinaire, and of course, it goes without saying, Trip-Out Empress. All the little windows that Hooks was so fond of, giving onto nothing but the ugly wall across the way, were pushed open wide, so the two mutually despising lovers wouldn't suffocate to death.

She was still smiling. You see, she said. You really do love Lyuba. Why else would you be here, right?

Hand over the key, he said. I won't give you that again.

Oh, you'll give me more than that, honey. I'm here to be your guinea pig.

So what is it? The missing ingredient?

You seriously don't know? Well, if you don't know, no one does.

Just drop it an let's get this over with.

C'mon, you know what it is. You've known all along!

No.

Sure you do. You just haven't realized it yet. That you know.

Meanwhile he got to work, getting ready to cook. Like it was ordinary crystals.

Look, said Vera. Here's what fell in there that time. She held up a plastic bag of white powder. He took a sniff and raised his eyebrows inquiringly.

It's epená, Vera announced.

We took that?

Guess so, it was a gift from Nembo the lancer. To me. Nembo was awesome, remember?

No. How do you know it was that? An what's the third thing?

Well, afterwards I moved back into the flat with Vladimir. Just a fling, you know, it blew over quick. Some of the ones who'd had a taste kept comin around, pain in the ass. Maybe Vladimir's got something goin with them. But our other pal wants it all for himself . . . She hesitated a moment. I'm not sure if I can trust Brownie. I donno. After what he did. I might be on my own. She stomped her foot. You fucker! You left me back there!

Drop it, said Hooks.

So we started tryin to figure it out. We were in that flat for days. We sold Noh, the bird. For start-up funds. Do you even remember him, you piece of shit? You ran out on him too. You left him out on the street, like me, you shit!

Vera . . .

Shut up a minute! You won't talk with me on the phone. I come over, we have sex a couple times, sure, great . . . but you don't give a damn about me!

OK, here we go . . . he turned up the flame a little. After what happened in the hospital, doing the old work brought him back to life again. That and his decision. He would give it to them and then he and Lyuba were out of there.

Listen to me! I don't care. You mean nothing to me, you hear? I couldn't care less. Nothing can happen to me. Doesn't it even bother you that the kid was Brownie's?

What?

He turned and walked toward her. She backed away, smiling again.

Nah, just kiddin. I'm kidding! Brownie's useless in bed anyway. All he's good for is stealing. You're better, you hear?

Hooks turned back to the burners. He'd had enough of that wench. Her and her twisted love.

Anyways . . . the way we figured it out was there was still some left at Vladimir's place. He stole it. Here, she handed Hooks something yellow. He took a taste.

What is it?

Don't ask me, yaga or something he said. Some Hispanics smuggled it in. Made in Latin America.

Yaga, like Baba Yaga.

I guess. Remember how good we were together?

Yeah right.

Listen: Vladimir's just a foot soldier. You're the only one I'm tellin this, but he's over an out. The head nurse took him in. After she got a taste. She'd let that hospital burn to the ground to get ahold of the stuff, hah. She's out too, obviously.

Yeah right.

Listen now: I don't give a damn about Brownie. Not one bit! You're the one I love. We can leave together. With this right here.

The mixture began to bubble.

What's the third thing, hurry up.

We can go, the two of us. You an me, we're connected. More than you think!

What's the third thing?

Blood. It's your blood.

What? Hooks almost knocked over the apparatus.

Yeah, when I came at you in the kitchen that time, remember?

Yeah. I got cut.

I cut you, babe, I'm sorry! But that's it. We figured it out. We did tests. Lots. An it turns out it was blood! These days who's surprised? Maybe you're chemically different somehow. Could be, right? Does that sound irratio . . . irrotio, hmm?

Hooks just stood there.

Irrational? She finally got the word out.

So that's it, said Hooks, that's how come I see . . . he rubbed his eyes, talking into space . . . the blood from my eyes, that's why I see it, going up . . . an coming down . . . an the bliss.

Stop babbling. An hurry up. Gimme the knife!

He stood there, trying to digest it: So why my blood?

Nobody knows. Maybe it'll work, an if not . . . Sweetie. You look like an alchemist! It's a mystical wedding!

Are you out of your mind?

You sonuvabitch! Why did you leave me back there? I love you! Let's leave, the two of us, all right?

No.

You jerk, you jerk! I wasn't kidding, it was Brownie's kid. An guess what? Guess what, you asshole? They tested it! They took it from Lyuba an tested the kid to find out the ingredient. That's why all this! You shouldn't've been so stubborn.

No, said Hooks.

She dodged him, tried to run, but there was nowhere to go, she slipped free somehow, darted around the room, Hooks's shoulder bumped against the bulb hanging from the ceiling, it swung back and forth, he stood still . . . Vera, off in the corner now, lost in the shadows, he could barely see her . . . she was seriously afraid.

He sat down on a chair and watched the apparatus. Then he heard her:

I was kiddin just now. I was lying. Sorry! Everything I said just now was lies. But try to understand, you left me back there . . . are you still mad at me? she said. Can I come over there? You look like you're counting thoughts!

Why my blood?

So that's all that's on your mind? That's it? Forget it! Nobody knows why yours. You've just got to accept it. I was kidding before, it might be your kid. An even if it isn't, you're all assholes, so what difference does it make. The kid's a kid, who cares . . . whose it is . . . jerks, every one of you . . . now she was standing next to him, ever so lightly and tentatively . . . leaning her shoulder against him. And when he stayed, she sort of . . .

hugged him . . . a little.

Listen, they tested all kinds of stuff. Lyuba's blood too. She wouldn't've had to stay that long if you'd given in sooner. They knew they had to hook you good to get you to say yes. They know you're a hard sell. Stubborn! Like a mule . . . hey, she ran a finger over his chin, he ducked away . . . ooh, I like that! She spun around the room, warily keeping her distance, clapping her hands.

Really, there's nothing wrong with Lyuba, she's fine, I give you my word as a woman.

If you're a woman . . .

So I'm not? She clapped her hands next to his ear. Slid a foot forward. Leaped in the air, she knew he was watching. She looked like she was ready to do a somersault.

Yeah. You are. So're we gonna do this or what?

Hm, she said, picking up the knife. They had plenty of those around.

He held out his hand.

Uh-uh, she said. I wanna be sure, like last time. She sliced his cheek.

A few drops obligingly ran down his face and into the boiling mixture.

Oh my God, said Vera. Oh my God, if this is it . . .

An if it's not?

I love you, she laughed. An if it is . . . then this whole thing's even more insane than you think.

They waited for the crystals to cool. They knew plenty of people who measured their time doing nothing but.

She swallowed it, sat down. Stood up and walked around the room. No, she said. I'm getting, I'm starting to get pretty high, but this isn't it! It's not it, she said, walking over to him.

I'd like to hug you now. Right this second.

You sure it's not it?

You can tell right away. Don't you remember?

No way to forget.

So what do we do? he asked. Asked her. He knew she knew. And then he saw the tear. Peeling away from under one of her heavily made-up eyes. Then the other. It looked bizarre. So all of a sudden.

What do we do? she whispered. She took a step toward him, he bent out of the way and his shoulder bumped the wire again, making the bulb swing back and forth. He watched the shadows moving on the far wall.

They flickered like flames. He was tense.

Well, that's it, she said. Now we can't leave each other, ever. Now there's no way.

He saw her pick up a knife, waited for her to cut him again, but no, she dragged the blade across her palm, and as a slim wound opened up, she stretched out her arm and stroked his cheek on the spot he had bled from a moment ago. Stroking it wasn't enough, she had to scratch the wound a little.

That's right, she said, our blood mixed together that time, just a few drops. No one knows why it is.

She saw Hooks watching her, saw something growing inside him, a mean look in his eyes, something happening in his face.

No! she screamed . . . don't.

Hooks tensed up inside, then something inside him burst and he leaned back. Exhausted, he leaned back against the stove.

Meanwhile their combined blood silently and dependably went to work in the concoction.

You . . . she said, softly and accusingly. You were going to kill me, weren't you. I could tell. I knew it.

He stepped into the center of the room, took a breath in, deep breath out, and touched his finger to the bulb. He hissed, it was hot. Inspected his finger, nothing, he hadn't actually burned himself.

But you didn't! Vera said. An you never will now. You love me too much. You need me.

She burst out laughing. Not at him. But because she'd just been born again. Out of joy at the gift of life, one of the nine she'd been given, it made her laugh so hard you could see her pretty teeth. Her face was . . . covered in dust, from the plaster all over the room, it made her face look almost like a mask, with the tears and the smeared makeup too, the cobwebs from the corner she had backed into to hide from him . . . but she was howling with laughter. She was in the clear, she knew it. It would dawn on him. As soon as he realized he was addicted.

After all, she was . . . always had been pretty much everything but stupid. She knew the way males kicked in their stalls when they suddenly became aware of the wires tearing into their heart and brain, along with their lungs and liver. And of who was so skillfully tugging the wires as they silently sliced their body apart.

The crystals had cooled.

You want to try too?

No, he said. If this is it, I'm takin it with me, get them off my back. If not, I don't know. Anyone lays a hand on Lyuba I'll destroy them. I'm warnin you. You know I like you.

Well, well, well . . . just look what's come of our poisoned blood, she said. Let's stay together. Say yes before I'm totally gone. Don't close the door yet. You have no idea what it is. No idea.

As soon as she swallowed, they could both tell. Even him. They had it.

He started to wrap the rest in foil. It had hardened into a sort of clod.

Wait, she said, just think about it. They're waiting over at that guy's place, that guy you work with here. That stupid thief Brownie the asshole's still got debts. An the old scammer won't pay him a thing unless he gets his sample today. Don't be afraid of me. Or for me. I'm wasted. We need each other. Jesus, I'm flying. It's beautiful.

Sit down on the chair, he told her.

She sat.

You're going to make my wish come true, she said, smiling

blissfully. I know you will. Whenever I want, dear friend. I
know what you want to do now. The things are telling me. So
go on an do it. I'll manage somehow. Just do it.

You bet I will . . . an sorry, he brushed past her out into the
hallway and slammed the door shut, the heavy, metal-plated
door, didn't hear a sound from Vera, not even when he turned
the key. Then he heard her but knew he had no choice, he took
the last few stairs at a leap and heard her, wondering how it
was possible, through all those old walls and the door, and it
sounded like wailing at first, then laughter, ringing in his ears,
echoing inside him . . . but he had to do it, he had no choice,
an she knows I have no choice, he thought, outside, walking
toward the gutter with the key in his hand . . . anyway I'm
sure that pussycat'll slip out of there somehow, she'll find a way
outta that hole, but as for me . . . I won't be around to see it . . .
he tossed the key down the sewer. It jingled. Clicked. Hooks
shuddered. Listened. But it was quiet.

He knew he would go to the intersection, and was glad that
it was dark, he would bypass the spot and go to where they were
waiting for him. He had the stuff wrapped in foil in his pocket,
he would give it to them and walk away, back to Lyuba, he
thought. He thought at the time.

He looked up at the sky. It was a very gloomy sky, and the
city was pulling it down toward itself, mangling it with electric
shocks and toxins from its incinerators, the city pulled the sky
down over it with great force, and there was nothing but some
fucking streetlamps shining and lifeless laser beams flashing,
and the haunted eyes of wandering robots, fugitives from
justice, burning into the sky . . . the foil with the stuff was in his
pocket, he put his hand over it, kept walking.

19. She Walked

NADIA WANTED OUT. Where to didn't matter. She left because she couldn't stand that woman anymore. She knew the woman was evil and that she would do her harm.

She had brought home some strange person and shut Nadia in the bathroom. Then Nadia heard her scream at the man. They hadn't locked her in, she'd escaped, dashing past them, they grabbed at her, but she got away. She knew her spell had killed the woman. But the woman had returned. She must've known a stronger spell. Nadia shrugged.

She came to the intersection. And suddenly felt uneasy. She closed her eyes to keep from seeing the people. She would have squeezed in between the buildings if she could have. If she could have moved. If the buildings had moved. She knew she was standing at the edge of a drop-off and if she took a step she'd go plunging down. Down into the pit, where her body would shatter to pieces. She didn't know whether to take that step.

Just then, something touched her, light and gentle, on her left shoulder. She opened her eyes. Saw through the people, to the other side. And there stood the old lady. In the middle of all the people, she didn't say anything, didn't wave to Nadia, nothing. But it was her.

Nadia was flooded with joy. She was no longer afraid. Then the old lady nodded to her. Nadia understood, she didn't have to say a word. She knew the old lady had been with her the whole time she was gone. And she knew, too, why it had to be that way. She knew what the old lady wanted.

Nadia moved on the inside first, then took a step. And another. Nothing happened, she didn't fall. She didn't fall down. What she wanted most at that moment was to run to the old lady, but she knew she shouldn't.

She walked, and the pavement beneath her feet was solid. Now Nadia knew what would happen. The old lady had told her what had to happen. But she had also told her that after that, nothing would ever hurt her again. No one would ever be able to harm her again. There was no way.

She looked at the old lady. She knew she would see her again later. The old lady nodded to her again. She was glad to see Nadia, glad that Nadia had understood. Then she vanished. Vanished into the crowd, there was no one there but the people.

Nadia turned around, walked. She walked, knowing what would happen. And she wasn't afraid. She was smiling. On the inside. She was looking forward to seeing the old lady again. And Mook too, she was looking forward a lot.

20. The Sky

HOOKS WAS SURPRISED at how Brownie was acting. The confident, know-it-all thug of not so long ago . . . now looked like a little boy.

The guy by the door, who'd let Hooks in, clearly had him in the palm of his hand. Brownie was whipped. Hooks grimaced to himself. Hadn't he told him to leave the cash alone? The guy was a fanatic, you don't mess with people like that. But he hadn't pulled down the grille behind him, Hooks made a mental note. It seemed important. He didn't like the look of things here. He wanted out ASAP. He still had the piece, wrapped in foil, in his pocket. The guy didn't talk to either of them. But he didn't object to Hooks's presence.

Maybe the best thing to do was just toss the foil on the table and get out. Back to Lyuba. Sell the buildings and get the hell out. Wherever. High time. They'd been living there too long already.

But there was still one question he wanted to ask Brownie. And he was amazed at how strong his hate was.

You got it? Where's Vera? his ex-buddy barked.

You scum! I told you how stupid it was stealin that cash from them. Sir, Hooks turned to the guy, my wife and I've got nothing to do with that money!

I know, the guy grumbled.

Where's Mr. Machata? Hooks asked.

You got it? Brownie said again, this time even more urgently.

Since when did you turn into such a fuckhead, anyway? said Hooks.

All right, fine, Brownie said. I borrowed some cash from

their company. Apparently Mr. Lurya here doesn't believe me. Neither does his lady friend. They've been holdin me here for a couple of hours now an . . . Machata too. We've been waitin on you, for the sample. Believe me, I've never waited like this before. Not for you. Not anyone. I borrowed the money cause me an Vera needed it to get you set up. We were sure we'd figured it out. Soon as you gimme me the sample, I'll get enough from Machata to pay off my debt to this . . . individual. An everything'll be fine. At least I hope. Got a smoke?

Hm, said Hooks. What good is one lousy sample?

Oh, c'mon, said Brownie. You know it comes from you now.

So you just figured if it checked out, I'd go in on it with you guys? That I'd have to, right? Hooks noticed the cramp iron on the ground in front of him, nudged it with his shoe.

It checked out, didn't it? said Brownie from the chair.

Yeah, said Hooks. Where's Vladimir? Since when is the shopkeeper in on it? Doesn't strike me as his cup of tea.

It's not. But he's got money. An he wants more. You got it, right?

Hooks reached into his pocket. Tell me the truth: Where's Vladimir?

Brownie just peeled back his lips in a grin.

Christ, he looks like a monster, Hooks thought. Christ, he is a monster. Hooks's throat was bone-dry. You could've heard if he had swallowed.

Listen, he said. That kid . . . Lyuba's, was it yours? Could it've been yours?

You got it?

Brownie hadn't expected him to drop a bomb like that. Even Hooks didn't understand what had gotten into him. But next thing he knew he was pressed up against the door in the hall where Lurya had shoved him. He stood watching as Lurya lifted Brownie up off the ground. Look out! he was going to shout. But before he could say it, in one swift motion Lurya knocked the knife from Brownie's hand. Then he set him back down in the chair. None too gently.

Hooks would've been happy to continue the conversation, but just then the door to the bathroom opened. Someone had knocked it open, probably with a kick.

His jaw dropped. He caught a glimpse of Machata sitting on the edge of the tub, stripped to his waist. Just sitting there. There was something in the tub. Clothes or something. And the cleaning lady! It took a moment for Hooks to recognize her. It was Machata's ex-wife.

But she was a far cry from the woman he'd met in the hospital. She stood there, haggard, all done up in some bizarre outfit, head wrapped in a bandanna, face sharp and narrow, she looked like some kind of freakish bird. And a mean one too. Her clothes were wet, Hooks noticed. He could see her eyes shining. He slid his gaze to Machata. His eyes were all glassy, face swollen and puffy. Like after an autopsy. Only Hooks had a hunch this was no autopsy. Not this, not now. That's not how it looked.

The woman silently entered the room, a puddle trailing behind her like a bedraggled train.

Hello, said Hooks. It was how he'd been raised.

Watch out for her, Brownie said quietly.

He didn't have to tell Hooks twice. The woman stood there, ten feet away, by the open door to the bathroom, and he could see it in her eyes. She wasn't looking at them, but into them and through them. She's insane, he thought. She must be insane. To his surprise and disgust, he realized he was afraid of her. An why wasn't Machata moving? An what was in the tub, he wondered. Then it dawned on him. What it was, what it had to be. I want out of here, he said loudly.

Brownie gave a feeble laugh.

Me too, for a good couple hours. Now give me it. I know you've got it. You have to have it. Please.

If I do, will they let me go? asked Hooks. He didn't move.

Of course, said the woman. She looks like she's made of wax,

Hooks thought. Like a puppet. An her voice is weird too. He was practically ready to whimper.

Of course, she repeated. Give it to him, it's his. He committed sins for it.

You, said Hooks. Do you know what this is about? he asked the woman.

We don't want it from you. We want it from him. Let him give it to us. We want it from him, because it caused him to sin. Against us.

For God's sake, Brownie wailed, just give it here so I can be in la-la land already, cough up the bliss, I don't care if the loonies rip me wide open . . . c'mon!

Hooks shuffled his feet, it dawned on him that, in this state, Brownie wouldn't give it to them anyway. But, after all, that was really none of his business. Let them fight over it, what did he care. All right, he said. And tossed it to him.

Brownie tore off the foil. And swallowed the chunk. Whole.

Are you crazy? yelled Hooks. Then it dawned on him. Why he'd eaten it whole. He had no intention of handing it over. He wanted to be gone, as far gone as possible, and fast.

Lurya gently lifted Brownie out of the chair, like a child, and set his limp body down in the corner of the room. Tugged on the zipper and opened his leather jacket. The woman walked over to him and kneeled down on the floor. In front of Brownie.

Hooks wanted no part of this, absolutely not. He didn't even want to see it. He wanted out. But first he went into the bathroom. Machata nodded in greeting. Hooks realized the reason his eyes were puffy was from crying. Machata rose heavily as Hooks came through the door.

She was lying in the tub. Grooves around her tiny neck. Eyes closed. The tub was filled with water, at least that's what Hooks thought it was. Till he noticed the canisters.

It had to be this way, said Machata softly.

Bastards, murderers, psychos . . . who did this? he heard himself say.

Who did this, Machata repeated after him.

Suddenly Hooks felt sorry for him. Painfully sorry. Couldn't've been this idiot, staggerin around like he's half-dead. That lady must've done it. Machata may be a jerk an a crook, but this . . . anyway, Hooks thought, it's curtains for him. He's dead meat. No way those two're letting him walk . . . an what about me?

She did it? he asked Machata softly.

She did it, the man repeated after him.

Now listen to me, said Hooks, trying not to look at the tiny body, the rags swollen with water, or whatever it was sloshing around in the tub, and the face . . . the little girl's face was submerged underwater. And those two, next door, whatever they were doing, Hooks heard a sound like fabric tearing, but otherwise it was quiet. Over there.

Listen, said Hooks, speaking quickly now, if it'd been you, if it'd been you who'd tortured her, I'd have to . . . I'd have to kill you now. I wouldn't be able to leave. An I want to. I'd have to kill you for that, I want you to know!

I want you to know, Machata repeated, but then he must have understood, because he laughed. And when Hooks heard that laugh, he had a feeling it was all over, he was losing his mind. The little girl lying in there, it had happened. This happened, Hooks thought with a fresh dose of horror, but he must have also said it out loud, because Machata moved his lips and said: This happened.

Then Machata struck a match and Hooks jumped out of the way and slammed his back against the door, dodging the burst of flames, through the wall of fire he caught a glimpse of Nadia's face, dead and calm amid the suddenly blazing water, a geyser of flames shot out of the tub, engulfing Machata too, covering him in the blink of an eye, he staggered, dazed, through the field of flames . . . but Hooks was already off and running, barreling across the room, he almost tripped over Brownie's legs, nearly knocked the woman over, Lurya swung at him, but Hooks flew down the hallway, and next thing he knew he was on the other side of the grille, he could feel the pavement underfoot . . . and stopped.

He stopped, turned, went back, in a single step stretched under the grille and into the shop, grabbed the hook from the front room, right there where it always was, saw smoke and heard voices from the hall, the woman screaming, maybe they were . . . Hooks grabbed a canister and tearing off the cap with the tip of the hook splashed benzene all over the shelves, then cracked open another one, flung the liquid on a pile of brushes, grabbed one more, ripped off the cap with his teeth, and then, through the smoke in the hall he saw Lurya gasping for breath, choking, his head was all that Hooks could see, he was crawling on all fours, and then he saw Brownie's head and shoulders, his old pal's body being dragged . . . and the lighter was in his hand and the fire came shooting out . . . and then he was back outside, tugging down the grille with the hook, hanging on it with his whole body, pulling with all his might, and the shutter slammed to the ground and Hooks hung from the bars. With both hands. Hung there. Breathing. Just breathing. He thought he heard voices and then the scrape of fingernails on metal, or maybe more like metal on metal, he heard the crackle and roar of flames, but he must've just imagined it, because look how thick that metal slab was, thing was solid metal . . . but if the flames had parted and the woman had suddenly appeared and said: Now you die, it would've happened, he knew it. But there was no one in sight. It was dark out.

So he walked downhill, he had to get to the intersection. He could sense it was getting light and he wanted to be there. At the spot. He would stand there till it started falling. Or something happened. After that, he would go find her, Lyuba, and they would leave. If she wasn't still in pain. He threw away the hook. His palms were scorched.

Now he stood at the intersection. Angel Exit, stood there waiting. And it came, sunup. The bloody orb, as usual, again sent forth its messengers to kill Hooks through his eyes. Kill him there, among the first morning pedestrians.

Then it happened, he took a deep breath . . . from down in his guts, there were things happening to him . . . and the pit wasn't there. He stood staring into the sun and the sky over Angel was red. He knew by now the fire in the building must've already consumed the bodies and the walls would be caving in soon and it would go shooting up to the sky. Uniting with the fiery glow of the heavens.

The sky was red, covered in blood, and it blazed above the old streets, searing the rot and filth out of them, the blood in the sky fed on the pain and gave it right back. It didn't frighten him. He felt something moving inside him, like love or something. Like a whirlpool. He reached in there, fished around, grabbed hold, and yanked. He felt fiercely. It was a new era, like the first day of the beginning of everything. He knew this was what he was going to feel from now on. For that street, that city, those people. In spite of it all. And what with everything. Then he made a move, here we go, it's time . . . he moved, bent over, touched the pavement.

THE END

Translator's Note

This is an exciting moment for readers of Central European literature. With the publication of *Angel Station*, my translation of the 1995 novel *Anděl*, all of Jáchym Topol's book-length works of fiction are now available in English.

From the outset, Topol distinguished himself as a writer with a singular voice and personality. His first book, the poetry collection *Miluju tě k zbláznění* (*I Love You Madly*), published in samizdat in 1988, was honored with the Tom Stoppard Prize. His most recent work, the novel *Chladnou zemí* (2009; English translation *The Devil's Workshop*, 2013), received the prestigious Jaroslav Seifert Prize, and in 2015 he was named the recipient of the Vilenica International Literary Prize, joining the ranks of such giants as Milan Kundera, Zbigniew Herbert, László Krasznahorkai, and Dubravka Ugrešić. The Slovenian author Alenka Jensterle Doležal, in her laudation, pronounced, "Like Hašek, Kafka and Hrabal, Jáchym Topol has left a permanent stamp on Central European literature."

Angel Station follows Topol's first two works of fiction—*Výlet k nádražní hale* (1993; English translation *A Trip to the Train Station*, 1995) and *Sestra* (1994; English translation *City Sister Silver*, 2000)—as the final panel in a prose triptych depicting the city of Prague and its inhabitants in the years just before and after the death of communism in the East bloc. Although different in structure (and in length) from its predecessors, it has a great deal in common with them in terms of themes and language.

Czech scholar Ivo Říha, in his afterword to the 2011 edition of *A Trip*, wrote of the author "opening wounds that remain open in his later works." Fear, desperation, and mental illness; addiction, corruption, and violence; filth and decay: these are the hallmarks of the society Topol shows us. "Nothing too pretty," says the unnamed narrator in Topol's first work of fiction. Like most of his protagonists (I'd hesitate to call them "heroes"), he is a loner looking for moral guidance and a place where he can belong. Here he is in a characteristically touching yet tongue-in-cheek exchange with a Greek chorus at the story's conclusion (even typeset as a drama):

Me: I'm trying I'm living
and I just had myself a little walk
through town and I think
I'll keep my hands clean and if not
then just a little bit dirty.

City Sister Silver, Topol's first true novel, covered far more ground, in every sense, than *A Trip*. (Which isn't surprising, given how much longer it is: a quarter million words, as opposed to the eighty-four hundred of its predecessor.) But it too features a narrator trying to "keep his hands clean" and failing pretty miserably. Like most of the other characters, lost amid the chaos of early post-communism, lacking support from family, school, religion, and other social institutions, Potok is a man in search of a tribe, people he can lean on: ". . . because not even the Church is older than the tribe, and we were closer to each other than to those broken-backed families of ours." This was in fact the experience that shaped Topol himself, growing up in the milieu of the 1970s and 1980s Czech underground, and even as his writing moved on to other topics, set in other places and time periods, it has remained a thematic anchor.

The absence of family as a source of grounding and identity is prominent in *Angel Station*. Here, for example, is Hooks, the story's narrator, describing his early childhood: "As for the parents he had once so eagerly watched from his crib—in a family of the type: father, mother, child (him)—he washed his hands of them before you could say 'toy boat' three times fast." Later, when his new neighbor, Lyuba, moves into the flat next to his, she informs him that the previous tenant has died and that it was her mother. He offers his condolences, but Lyuba says, "Her death means nothing to me. Maybe later I'll feel it." Hooks comments, to the reader: "If she did, she never said so."

Although "open wounds" and dysfunction are most visible in Topol's characters and the relationships between them, they are also present in the environment, both natural and built. Says the narrator of *A Trip*: "Some streets still made you feel like the best thing to do was drug yourself till you dropped. And there were corners, dark and damp with black sewer water, where you could come down with schizophrenia as easily as you catch a cold." *City Sister Silver* is peppered with references to pollution and its impact on human and animal habitats alike: "the fetid Moldau," "the smog-choked wolves," "the nastiest toxic factories," "A pool clouded with chemicals, unrippled by worms." In *Angel Station* we read of the "chemical sky writhing up above," "condemned ruins and demolitions," "toxins from [the city's] incinerators," and, recalling the generations of Czech Jews killed in the Holocaust (a nod to the recurring theme of genocide in Topol's works), an abandoned synagogue, where Hooks, passing by, "could smell the urine. How many generations of drunks had pissed there since the war. Under the archway, against the battered door."

Those reading this note after they've finished the book will already know that the title *Angel Station* comes from the name of the area around the intersection in the Prague district of

Smíchov where most of the novel's action takes place, and is also the name of the Prague Metro station located there. Topol had an apartment in the neighborhood for years, and during the early 1990s, when I lived in Prague, I visited him there often—including my fair share of outings to Klamovka, "the pub on the hill." Although the Smíchov Synagogue has been preserved, construction of the three-story Nový Smíchov shopping mall, in 2001, changed the area almost beyond recognition. In fact some of the last images of the old Anděl intersection and its environs were captured in the 2000 feature film *Anděl Exit*, based on Topol's novel, with a screenplay by him, directed by Vladimír Michálek.

***

Topol's renown as an author, both at home and abroad, stems as much from his use of language as it does from his subject matter. His early writings, in his teen years, took the form of song lyrics and poems, and even as a prose writer, the word-to-word progression of his sentences is heavily determined by rhythm and sound. This, along with his penchant for mixing high and low registers, is the distinguishing feature of his style, carried forward from his poetry into all his works of fiction, including this one. "The sky was red. It was dazzling. He tried to move, felt a drip, drop, drip on his shoulders, neck, scalp, knew it was blood." One can easily imagine these sentences typeset on the page as verse (and in fact there are several places in *Angel Station* where Topol composes his text as poetry).

One of the greatest challenges for the translator is to resist the temptation to "smooth out" or "normalize" Topol's language. Although less in this novel than in *City Sister Silver*, in addition to using features of Czech particular to Prague, he also makes heavy use of *obecná* ("colloquial") and *hovorová* ("spoken") Czech, and not only in dialogue, where one would typically expect it. In English these can come across as ethnic or socioeconomic class markers, whereas in Czech they are more a reflection of the social context: Even upper-class or highly educated Czechs typically use spoken or colloquial language with family, friends, or peers when not in public. In translating *City Sister Silver*, I wrote the dialogue in English following Topol's model, writing words as people pronounced them. I also respected his convention of not using quotation marks, and chose to drop letters, as he did, instead of replacing them with apostrophes, since I felt it would have made the text appear more old-fashioned and suggest a patronizing attitude toward the characters, which Topol decidedly didn't have. This translation of mine is appearing sixteen years after *City Sister Silver*. In Czech, though, *Anděl* was published the year after *Sestra*, so the lineage between the two is direct and clear, and it was important to me to preserve that relationship in my translation, too, by applying the same approach in this book.

One last strand of kinship between Topol's first three works of prose, in addition to the recurring themes and stylistic features: There are two minor characters in this novel who may be familiar to hardcore Topol fans. Činča made his first appearance in *A Trip to the Train Station* (Topol memorably described the name to me as the sound of a knife slashing in and out of flesh), and Čáp, mentioned just once in *Angel Station*, is the curly-haired, cobblestone-throwing activist from *City Sister Silver* ("Čáp's teachings were more and more appealing every day, because he knew the war against communism must lead also to the liberation of ants and every living creature, that no one must harm the helpless and the young, and that whosoever does must accept the punishment . . . only his kingdom was a kingdom not of this world.")

In theme and language, then, *Angel Station* shares a great deal with the two books that Topol wrote before it. But, unlike the zigzag day-or-two-in-the-life of *A Trip to the Train Station* and the sprawling labyrinth of *City Sister Silver*, this time out Topol produced a much more "normal" novel in terms of both structure and length, with a plot that follows a relatively straightforward arc: "Man in Hole," to use the term from Kurt Vonnegut's famously rejected master's thesis on the simple shapes of stories. (As he summed it up: "Somebody gets into trouble, gets out of it again.")

***

As I write this, I've got three chapters in my computer from a new novel Topol is working on now, titled *Citlivý člověk* (Sensitive person). The first sentence reads, "The D1 highway, glossy with rain, cuts across the landscape." I can't wait to see where that road goes.

Alex Zucker
Brooklyn, NY
September 2016

Jáchym Topol is the author of novels, poetry, stories, dramas, screenplays, reportage, and song lyrics. His novel *City Sister Silver* was listed *1001 Books You Should Read Before You Die*.

In 2013, he was awarded an English PEN award for writing in translation. He is the winner of the Vilenica International Literary Prize, and two of the most prestigious Czech literary awards, the Tom Stoppard Prize, and the Jaroslav Seifert Prize.

Alex Zucker is the translator of three previous books by Jáchym Topol, as well as novels by Tomáš Zmeškal, Magdaléna Platzová, Josef Jedlička, Heda Margolius Kovály, Petra Hůlová, Patrik Ouředník, and Miloslava Holubová.

MICHAL AJVAZ, *The Golden Age.*
The Other City.

PIERRE ALBERT-BIROT, *Grabinoulor.*

YUZ ALESHKOVSKY, *Kangaroo.*

FELIPE ALFAU, *Chromos.*
Locos.

JOE AMATO, *Samuel Taylor's Last Night.*

IVAN ÂNGELO, *The Celebration.*
The Tower of Glass.

ANTÓNIO LOBO ANTUNES, *Knowledge of Hell.*
The Splendor of Portugal.

ALAIN ARIAS-MISSON, *Theatre of Incest.*

JOHN ASHBERY & JAMES SCHUYLER,
A Nest of Ninnies.

ROBERT ASHLEY, *Perfect Lives.*

GABRIELA AVIGUR-ROTEM, *Heatwave and Crazy Birds.*

DJUNA BARNES, *Ladies Almanack.*
Ryder.

JOHN BARTH, *Letters.*
Sabbatical.

DONALD BARTHELME, *The King.*
Paradise.

SVETISLAV BASARA, *Chinese Letter.*

MIQUEL BAUÇÀ, *The Siege in the Room.*

RENÉ BELLETTO, *Dying.*

MAREK BIENCZYK, *Transparency.*

ANDREI BITOV, *Pushkin House.*

ANDREJ BLATNIK, *You Do Understand.*
Law of Desire.

LOUIS PAUL BOON, *Chapel Road.*
My Little War.
Summer in Termuren.

ROGER BOYLAN, *Killoyle.*

IGNÁCIO DE LOYOLA BRANDÃO,
Anonymous Celebrity.
Zero.

BONNIE BREMSER, *Troia: Mexican Memoirs.*

CHRISTINE BROOKE-ROSE,
Amalgamemnon.

BRIGID BROPHY, *In Transit.*
The Prancing Novelist.

GERALD L. BRUNS,
Modern Poetry and the Idea of Language.

GABRIELLE BURTON, *Heartbreak Hotel.*

MICHEL BUTOR, *Degrees.*
Mobile.

G. CABRERA INFANTE, *Infante's Inferno.*
Three Trapped Tigers.

JULIETA CAMPOS, *The Fear of Losing Eurydice.*

ANNE CARSON, *Eros the Bittersweet.*

ORLY CASTEL-BLOOM, *Dolly City.*

LOUIS-FERDINAND CÉLINE, *North.*
Conversations with Professor Y.
London Bridge.

MARIE CHAIX, *The Laurels of Lake Constance.*

HUGO CHARTERIS, *The Tide Is Right.*

ERIC CHEVILLARD, *Demolishing Nisard.*
The Author and Me.

MARC CHOLODENKO, *Mordechai Schamz.*

JOSHUA COHEN, *Witz.*

EMILY HOLMES COLEMAN, *The Shutter of Snow.*

ERIC CHEVILLARD, *The Author and Me.*

ROBERT COOVER, *A Night at the Movies.*

STANLEY CRAWFORD, *Log of the S.S. The Mrs Unguentine.*
Some Instructions to My Wife.

RENÉ CREVEL, *Putting My Foot in It.*

RALPH CUSACK, *Cadenza.*

NICHOLAS DELBANCO, *Sherbrookes.*
The Count of Concord.

NIGEL DENNIS, *Cards of Identity.*

PETER DIMOCK, *A Short Rhetoric for Leaving the Family.*

ARIEL DORFMAN, *Konfidenz.*

COLEMAN DOWELL, *Island People.*
Too Much Flesh and Jabez.

ARKADII DRAGOMOSHCHENKO,
Dust.

RIKKI DUCORNET, *Phosphor in Dreamland.*
The Complete Butcher's Tales.

RIKKI DUCORNET (cont.), *The Jade Cabinet.*
The Fountains of Neptune.

WILLIAM EASTLAKE, *The Bamboo Bed.*
Castle Keep.
Lyric of the Circle Heart.

JEAN ECHENOZ, *Chopin's Move.*

STANLEY ELKIN, *A Bad Man.*
Criers and Kibitzers, Kibitzers and Criers.
The Dick Gibson Show.
The Franchiser.
The Living End.
Mrs. Ted Bliss.

FRANÇOIS EMMANUEL, *Invitation to a Voyage.*

PAUL EMOND, *The Dance of a Sham.*

SALVADOR ESPRIU, *Ariadne in the Grotesque Labyrinth.*

LESLIE A. FIEDLER, *Love and Death in the American Novel.*

JUAN FILLOY, *Op Oloop.*

ANDY FITCH, *Pop Poetics.*

GUSTAVE FLAUBERT, *Bouvard and Pécuchet.*

KASS FLEISHER, *Talking out of School.*

JON FOSSE, *Aliss at the Fire.*
Melancholy.

FORD MADOX FORD, *The March of Literature.*

MAX FRISCH, *I'm Not Stiller.*
Man in the Holocene.

CARLOS FUENTES, *Christopher Unborn.*
Distant Relations.
Terra Nostra.
Where the Air Is Clear.

TAKEHIKO FUKUNAGA, *Flowers of Grass.*

WILLIAM GADDIS, JR., *The Recognitions.*

JANICE GALLOWAY, *Foreign Parts.*
The Trick Is to Keep Breathing.

WILLIAM H. GASS, *Life Sentences.*
The Tunnel.
The World Within the Word.
Willie Masters' Lonesome Wife.

GÉRARD GAVARRY, *Hoppla! 1 2 3.*

ETIENNE GILSON, *The Arts of the Beautiful.*
Forms and Substances in the Arts.

C. S. GISCOMBE, *Giscome Road.*
Here.

DOUGLAS GLOVER, *Bad News of the Heart.*

WITOLD GOMBROWICZ, *A Kind of Testament.*

PAULO EMÍLIO SALES GOMES, *P's Three Women.*

GEORGI GOSPODINOV, *Natural Novel.*

JUAN GOYTISOLO, *Count Julian.*
Juan the Landless.
Makbara.
Marks of Identity.

HENRY GREEN, *Blindness.*
Concluding.
Doting.
Nothing.

JACK GREEN, *Fire the Bastards!*

JIŘÍ GRUŠA, *The Questionnaire.*

MELA HARTWIG, *Am I a Redundant Human Being?*

JOHN HAWKES, *The Passion Artist.*
Whistlejacket.

ELIZABETH HEIGHWAY, ED.,
Contemporary Georgian Fiction.

AIDAN HIGGINS, *Balcony of Europe.*
Blind Man's Bluff.
Bornholm Night-Ferry.
Langrishe, Go Down.
Scenes from a Receding Past.

KEIZO HINO, *Isle of Dreams.*

KAZUSHI HOSAKA, *Plainsong.*

ALDOUS HUXLEY, *Antic Hay.*
Point Counter Point.
Those Barren Leaves.
Time Must Have a Stop.

NAOYUKI II, *The Shadow of a Blue Cat.*

DRAGO JANČAR, *The Tree with No Name.*

MIKHEIL JAVAKHISHVILI, *Kvachi.*

GERT JONKE, *The Distant Sound.*
Homage to Czerny.
The System of Vienna.

JACQUES JOUET, *Mountain R.*
Savage.
Upstaged.
MIEKO KANAI, *The Word Book.*
YORAM KANIUK, *Life on Sandpaper.*
ZURAB KARUMIDZE, *Dagny.*
JOHN KELLY, *From Out of the City.*
HUGH KENNER, *Flaubert, Joyce
and Beckett: The Stoic Comedians.*
Joyce's Voices.
DANILO KIŠ, *The Attic.*
The Lute and the Scars.
Psalm 44.
A Tomb for Boris Davidovich.
ANITA KONKKA, *A Fool's Paradise.*
GEORGE KONRÁD, *The City Builder.*
TADEUSZ KONWICKI, *A Minor
Apocalypse.*
The Polish Complex.
ANNA KORDZAIA-SAMADASHVILI,
Me, Margarita.
MENIS KOUMANDAREAS, *Koula.*
ELAINE KRAF, *The Princess of 72nd Street.*
JIM KRUSOE, *Iceland.*
AYSE KULIN, *Farewell: A Mansion in
Occupied Istanbul.*
EMILIO LASCANO TEGUI, *On Elegance
While Sleeping.*
ERIC LAURRENT, *Do Not Touch.*
VIOLETTE LEDUC, *La Bâtarde.*
EDOUARD LEVÉ, *Autoportrait.*
Newspaper.
Suicide.
Works.
MARIO LEVI, *Istanbul Was a Fairy Tale.*
DEBORAH LEVY, *Billy and Girl.*
JOSÉ LEZAMA LIMA, *Paradiso.*
ROSA LIKSOM, *Dark Paradise.*
OSMAN LINS, *Avalovara.*
The Queen of the Prisons of Greece.
FLORIAN LIPUŠ, *The Errors of Young Tjaž.*
GORDON LISH, *Peru.*
ALF MACLOCHLAINN, *Out of Focus.*
Past Habitual.

The Corpus in the Library.
RON LOEWINSOHN, *Magnetic Field(s).*
YURI LOTMAN, *Non-Memoirs.*
D. KEITH MANO, *Take Five.*
MINA LOY, *Stories and Essays of Mina Loy.*
MICHELINE AHARONIAN MARCOM,
A Brief History of Yes.
The Mirror in the Well.
BEN MARCUS, *The Age of Wire and String.*
WALLACE MARKFIELD, *Teitlebaum's
Window.*
DAVID MARKSON, *Reader's Block.*
Wittgenstein's Mistress.
CAROLE MASO, *AVA.*
HISAKI MATSUURA, *Triangle.*
LADISLAV MATEJKA & KRYSTYNA
POMORSKA, EDS., *Readings in Russian
Poetics: Formalist & Structuralist Views.*
HARRY MATHEWS, *Cigarettes.*
The Conversions.
The Human Country.
The Journalist.
My Life in CIA.
Singular Pleasures.
The Sinking of the Odradek.
Stadium.
Tlooth.
HISAKI MATSUURA, *Triangle.*
DONAL MCLAUGHLIN, *beheading the
virgin mary, and other stories.*
JOSEPH MCELROY, *Night Soul and
Other Stories.*
ABDELWAHAB MEDDEB, *Talismano.*
GERHARD MEIER, *Isle of the Dead.*
HERMAN MELVILLE, *The Confidence-
Man.*
AMANDA MICHALOPOULOU, *I'd Like.*
STEVEN MILLHAUSER, *The Barnum
Museum.*
In the Penny Arcade.
RALPH J. MILLS, JR., *Essays on Poetry.*
MOMUS, *The Book of Jokes.*
CHRISTINE MONTALBETTI, *The Origin
of Man.*
Western.

NICHOLAS MOSLEY, *Accident.*
Assassins.
Catastrophe Practice.
A Garden of Trees.
Hopeful Monsters.
Imago Bird.
Inventing God.
Look at the Dark.
Metamorphosis.
Natalie Natalia.
Serpent.
WARREN MOTTE, *Fables of the Novel:*
French Fiction since 1990.
Fiction Now: The French Novel in the
21st Century.
Mirror Gazing.
Oulipo: A Primer of Potential Literature.
GERALD MURNANE, *Barley Patch.*
Inland.
YVES NAVARRE, *Our Share of Time.*
Sweet Tooth.
DOROTHY NELSON, *In Night's City.*
Tar and Feathers.
ESHKOL NEVO, *Homesick.*
WILFRIDO D. NOLLEDO, *But for*
the Lovers.
BORIS A. NOVAK, *The Master of*
Insomnia.
FLANN O'BRIEN, *At Swim-Two-Birds.*
The Best of Myles.
The Dalkey Archive.
The Hard Life.
The Poor Mouth.
The Third Policeman.
CLAUDE OLLIER, *The Mise-en-Scène.*
Wert and the Life Without End.
PATRIK OUŘEDNÍK, *Europeana.*
The Opportune Moment, 1855.
BORIS PAHOR, *Necropolis.*
FERNANDO DEL PASO, *News from*
the Empire.
Palinuro of Mexico.
ROBERT PINGET, *The Inquisitory.*
Mahu or The Material.
Trio.
MANUEL PUIG, *Betrayed by Rita*
Hayworth.

The Buenos Aires Affair.
Heartbreak Tango.
RAYMOND QUENEAU, *The Last Days.*
Odile.
Pierrot Mon Ami.
Saint Glinglin.
ANN QUIN, *Berg.*
Passages.
Three.
Tripticks.
ISHMAEL REED, *The Free-Lance*
Pallbearers.
The Last Days of Louisiana Red.
Ishmael Reed: The Plays.
Juice!
The Terrible Threes.
The Terrible Twos.
Yellow Back Radio Broke-Down.
JASIA REICHARDT, *15 Journeys Warsaw*
to London.
JOÃO UBALDO RIBEIRO, *House of the*
Fortunate Buddhas.
JEAN RICARDOU, *Place Names.*
RAINER MARIA RILKE,
The Notebooks of Malte Laurids Brigge.
JULIÁN RÍOS, *The House of Ulysses.*
Larva: A Midsummer Night's Babel.
Poundemonium.
ALAIN ROBBE-GRILLET, *Project for a*
Revolution in New York.
A Sentimental Novel.
AUGUSTO ROA BASTOS, *I the Supreme.*
DANIËL ROBBERECHTS, *Arriving in*
Avignon.
JEAN ROLIN, *The Explosion of the*
Radiator Hose.
OLIVIER ROLIN, *Hotel Crystal.*
ALIX CLEO ROUBAUD, *Alix's Journal.*
JACQUES ROUBAUD, *The Form of*
a City Changes Faster, Alas, Than the
Human Heart.
The Great Fire of London.
Hortense in Exile.
Hortense Is Abducted.
Mathematics: The Plurality of Worlds of
Lewis.
Some Thing Black.

RAYMOND ROUSSEL, *Impressions of Africa.*

VEDRANA RUDAN, *Night.*

PABLO M. RUIZ, *Four Cold Chapters on the Possibility of Literature.*

GERMAN SADULAEV, *The Maya Pill.*

TOMAŽ ŠALAMUN, *Soy Realidad.*

LYDIE SALVAYRE, *The Company of Ghosts.*
The Lecture.
The Power of Flies.

LUIS RAFAEL SÁNCHEZ, *Macho Camacho's Beat.*

SEVERO SARDUY, *Cobra & Maitreya.*

NATHALIE SARRAUTE, *Do You Hear Them?*
Martereau.
The Planetarium.

STIG SÆTERBAKKEN, *Siamese.*
Self-Control.
Through the Night.

ARNO SCHMIDT, *Collected Novellas.*
Collected Stories.
Nobodaddy's Children.
Two Novels.

ASAF SCHURR, *Motti.*

GAIL SCOTT, *My Paris.*

DAMION SEARLS, *What We Were Doing and Where We Were Going.*

JUNE AKERS SEESE,
Is This What Other Women Feel Too?

BERNARD SHARE, *Inish.*
Transit.

VIKTOR SHKLOVSKY, *Bowstring.*
Literature and Cinematography.
Theory of Prose.
Third Factory.
Zoo, or Letters Not about Love.

PIERRE SINIAC, *The Collaborators.*

KJERSTI A. SKOMSVOLD,
The Faster I Walk, the Smaller I Am.

JOSEF ŠKVORECKÝ, *The Engineer of Human Souls.*

GILBERT SORRENTINO, *Aberration of Starlight.*
Blue Pastoral.
Crystal Vision.

Imaginative Qualities of Actual Things.
Mulligan Stew. Red the Fiend.
Steelwork.
Under the Shadow.

MARKO SOSIČ, *Ballerina, Ballerina.*

ANDRZEJ STASIUK, *Dukla.*
Fado.

GERTRUDE STEIN, *The Making of Americans.*
A Novel of Thank You.

LARS SVENDSEN, *A Philosophy of Evil.*

PIOTR SZEWC, *Annihilation.*

GONÇALO M. TAVARES, *A Man: Klaus Klump.*
Jerusalem.
Learning to Pray in the Age of Technique.

LUCIAN DAN TEODOROVICI,
Our Circus Presents...

NIKANOR TERATOLOGEN, *Assisted Living.*

STEFAN THEMERSON, *Hobson's Island.*
The Mystery of the Sardine.
Tom Harris.

TAEKO TOMIOKA, *Building Waves.*

JOHN TOOMEY, *Sleepwalker.*

DUMITRU TSEPENEAG, *Hotel Europa.*
The Necessary Marriage.
Pigeon Post.
Vain Art of the Fugue.

ESTHER TUSQUETS, *Stranded.*

DUBRAVKA UGRESIC, *Lend Me Your Character.*
Thank You for Not Reading.

TOR ULVEN, *Replacement.*

MATI UNT, *Brecht at Night.*
Diary of a Blood Donor.
Things in the Night.

ÁLVARO URIBE & OLIVIA SEARS, EDS.,
Best of Contemporary Mexican Fiction.

ELOY URROZ, *Friction.*
The Obstacles.

LUISA VALENZUELA, *Dark Desires and the Others.*
He Who Searches.

PAUL VERHAEGHEN, *Omega Minor.*

BORIS VIAN, *Heartsnatcher.*

FOR A FULL LIST OF PUBLICATIONS, VISIT: www.dalkeyarchive.com

LLORENÇ VILLALONGA, *The Dolls' Room.*

TOOMAS VINT, *An Unending Landscape.*

ORNELA VORPSI, *The Country Where No One Ever Dies.*

AUSTRYN WAINHOUSE, *Hedyphagetica.*

CURTIS WHITE, *America's Magic Mountain.*
The Idea of Home.
Memories of My Father Watching TV.
Requiem.

DIANE WILLIAMS,
Excitability: Selected Stories.
Romancer Erector.

DOUGLAS WOOLF, *Wall to Wall.*
Ya! & John-Juan.

JAY WRIGHT, *Polynomials and Pollen.*
The Presentable Art of Reading Absence.

PHILIP WYLIE, *Generation of Vipers.*

MARGUERITE YOUNG, *Angel in the Forest.*
Miss MacIntosh, My Darling.

REYOUNG, *Unbabbling.*

VLADO ŽABOT, *The Succubus.*

ZORAN ŽIVKOVIĆ , *Hidden Camera.*

LOUIS ZUKOFSKY, *Collected Fiction.*

VITOMIL ZUPAN, *Minuet for Guitar.*

SCOTT ZWIREN, *God Head.*

AND MORE . . .